Nikki Rae

Caught Up in a Thug's Heart

by

Nikki Rae

TP
Tyanna Presents

Caught Up in a Thug's heart
Copyright © 2021 by Nikki Rae
Published by Tyanna Presents
www.tyannapresents1@gmail.com
All rights reserved. No part of this book may be used
or used in reviews.
This is a work of fiction. Any references or similarities
to actual events, real people, living or dead, or to the
real locals intended to give the novel a sense of
reality. Any similarity in other names, characters,
places, and incidents are entirely coincidental

Nikki Rae

Synopsis

From the outside looking in, most people will think Olivia and Andrew have the perfect marriage, but that can't be further from the truth. Olivia wonders every day what has happened to the man she married. No matter how hard her marriage became, she tries to stay and make it work. At least, until she meets Shane.

Shane Hill is one of the youngest and largest street thugs in Camden. Shane has a daughter who is the only thing that comes before the streets. Women always held a temporary space in his life. But when he meets the one woman he can't have, suddenly, he wants something more permanent. The only thing standing in his way is age and her husband.

When Andrew pushes Olivia too far, will she run to Shane for help? Or, will she let the age difference between her and Shane keep her from a thug's love? Find out in this drama-filled urban romance *Caught Up in a Thug's Heart!*

Olivia

"Olivia, how long are you going to let this man treat you like this?" my best friend asked.

"Trish, it's not that easy to leave. He's my husband, and I love him," I told her.

"What does love have to do with this? This man belittles you. Not to mention, he's a cheating bastard. You just found out that you have chlamydia, and you're going to let that shit ride? All because he's your husband? Well, it's clear that he doesn't care that you're his wife."

"I didn't call you over here to be judged. You have no clue what it means to be married. I can't just walk away."

"Look, Liv, I'm not judging you. I just want better for you because I love you. But I don't want to know what marriage is like if I have to deal with what you deal with, just to say I have a husband."

Before I could respond, the door opened, and my husband, Andrew, walked in.

Trish rolled her eyes. "Look, I have to go. Just call me later."

When she walked out the door, Andrew walked into the living room where I was standing.

"What the hell is your face all ripped up for?" he asked.

"Well, I see I don't even get so much as a hello, but if you must know, my face is ripped up because I went to the doctor today, and you gave me chlamydia again, Andrew. It's not bad enough that you fuck around on me, but you have to burn me too?" I asked, getting emotional.

"Oliva, I'm not beat for this shit. I just got off of work, and as soon as I walk in, you start talking about some crazy shit. Did you cook dinner yet?" he questioned, disregarding my feelings.

"You know what, Andrew? Fuck you! Tell that bitch who gave you chlamydia to cook you dinner!" I yelled and walked into my bedroom.

I sat on the edge of the bed and just cried. I was starting to get tired of Andrew's shit and his disrespect.

My name is Olivia Palmer. I was born and raised in Camden, New Jersey, but I now lived in Gloucester City, New Jersey, which was just minutes away from Camden. I'm thirty-five years old and married with no kids.

I've been married to Andrew for five years. In the beginning, everything was good, and Andrew made me extremely happy. Shit didn't start getting rocky until last year after he asked for us to start a family. I was cool with that, but for some reason, I haven't gotten pregnant yet. It was hard conceiving when your husband was always on the road, doing God knows what with these nasty hoes who kept on giving him STDs.

Shit was rocky with us, and Andrew could care less. I was so unhappy within this marriage but didn't know how to leave. The truth was, I loved Andrew. I just wanted things to go back to what they used to be.

Andrew was the breadwinner of the house. He didn't want me to work, but I have always wanted to be a preschool teacher. I had just gotten my teacher's certificate just before I met Andrew, yet I never got to use it because he wanted me to be a housewife.

We got married within six months of dating. Andrew was five years older than I. Like a fool, I thought being with an older man was the way to go, but now, I wished I had taken my time and waited a little longer. Andrew was sweet when he wanted to be, but he was also cruel.

Once I got myself together, I walked out of the room, and Andrew was no longer here. I didn't even bother to call him because I was tired of caring.

***

The next morning when I woke up, Andrew wasn't in the bed. After I used the bathroom and handled my hygiene, I walked into the kitchen to make some coffee.

I was so tired of sitting in this damn house, all day, every day. If I wasn't hanging out with Trish, or out shopping for groceries, I was usually in the house doing nothing.

Once my coffee was done, I sat at the table and went through my emails. I ran across an email from three days ago about a teaching position that I'd applied for last month. I clicked on the email and got excited to see they wanted me to come in for an interview.

My heart dropped when I realized that it was for today *and* in the next half-hour. I cursed myself for not reading my emails sooner.

I didn't have any time to waste, so I ran into the room and tried to find something to wear. I pulled out a dress and some shoes, then I took a two-minute shower and threw on my clothes. My hair was already done, so I didn't have to worry about that. I didn't live far from the school, so after grabbing my business folder, I headed out the door.

The sun hit my face as soon as I walked outside. It was the end of the summer, so it was hot as hell.

I pulled up to Yorkship Elementary School in about ten minutes, just making it in time for my interview. I walked in and headed to the main office. Minutes later, the principal came out and called me into her office.

The interview didn't last long at all, and I was nervous because this was my first real interview. I loved her vibe, so I was comfortable and was now using my gift of gab to land the job I wanted so badly.

I loved kids and always have, which was why when Andrew mentioned having them, I was all for it. If I got this job, I would be so happy.

"Well, Mrs. Palmer. Normally, I would tell you I'd

call you back within the next couple of days, but after talking to you and hearing your excitement, not to mention, the love for kids in your voice, all I can say is, welcome aboard."

"Oh my God, are you serious? Thank you so much," I blurted. I was elated!

It was something that would help me take my mind off what I had going on at home with Andrew. Most importantly, it was something I wanted to do.

"You're more than welcome. Now you know that school starts in three weeks, but you will have to start next week, so you can get your classroom together. I will call you with an exact start date; we're still working out some stuff. But I will advise that you get your ideas together and go to the store and start purchasing things for your classroom."

That was all I needed to hear to get things in motion.

As soon as I got in my car, the first person I called was Trish, but she didn't answer. When I got home, I went on Pinterest to get some ideas.

Andrew

When I walked into the house last night, and my wife told me that I gave her an STD, I was pissed. I loved my wife to death, but I hated that we've been trying to get pregnant for a little over a year now, and we still haven't conceived.

I knew more than anything that I wanted a family, and I wanted it the right way. I wanted a wife and kids. Two would be good, but if we had more, then so be it.

I knew I didn't do right by Olivia and that I took

her for granted, but sometimes, it happened. When she told me she had chlamydia, I knew exactly who I'd gotten that shit from. So when she walked into the bedroom, I left out the door.

Minutes later, I pulled up to my destination. I jumped out of the car and knocked on the door like I was the damn police.

"Who is it?"

"Open this fucking door!"

When she opened the door, she looked surprised to see me. "Andrew, why the hell are you banging on my door like that? I have neighbors."

"Fuck you and your neighbors. Who the hell have you been fucking, Trish?"

"I'm not fucking anyone, but who the hell do you think you're talking to? Do I look like Olivia to you?"

"I don't give a fuck who you look like. You fucking burnt me."

"Andrew, I didn't burn you, so that means you're fucking someone other than Olivia and myself."

I had to think about what she said, then I remembered while I was in New York, I was fucking some chick when I was there.

"Look, you need to go to the doctor and take care

of that."

"Look, Andrew. I'm going to go get checked, but not for you. For the sake of Olivia, I can't mess with you like that anymore. What we're doing is fucked up, and Olivia is my best friend," Trish said, causing me to laugh. "What's so funny?"

"You're funny. You have the nerve to sit here and act like you're concerned about Olivia, yet you're smiling in her face, giving her relationship tips, all while fucking her husband?" I just shook my head.

"You know what? Fuck you, Andrew! We're done. You don't have to worry about me anymore. Just go!" she yelled.

I walked out her door, then got in my car and headed to a hotel. This was too much.

The name is Andrew Palmer, born and raised in Philadelphia, but I moved to Jersey about seven years ago. I'm about to be forty years old, and I've made a nice life for myself. Working as an architect, I traveled frequently and to a lot of different states.

I have the money, a wife, and the only thing I was missing was a kid.

Olivia was younger than I, but my wife was fine, and half of the time, I didn't know why I did the shit I did to her because she was a great woman. Olivia was beautiful with a body to die for.

The bitches I fucked with didn't have shit on my wife besides the fact that she couldn't give me a child.

I hated that I started fucking with her best friend, but that shit just kinda happened. It wasn't like she had anything on Olivia, but shit was just easier with her, and she was willing to fuck with me knowing what it was.

If my wife ever found out, she would lose it. Maybe it *was* a great idea to leave Trish alone. She wasn't worth losing Olivia over. In fact, none of them were. I really needed to get my shit together and start treating my wife the way she deserved to be treated. From here on out, I was going to work on my marriage and start acting like the husband she deserved.

I was on my way to the pharmacy to pick up my pills to get rid of this damn chlamydia. I knew I was playing with fire fucking around without using anything. I wouldn't be able to live with myself if I gave my wife something she couldn't get rid of.

After I picked up my medicine, I headed home. When I pulled up, I didn't see Olivia's car and wondered where she was. It was time that we talked. I went into the house and took my pills. I pulled out my cell and called my wife, but she didn't answer the phone. I sat down on the couch, and a few minutes later, Olivia walked in.

"Hey, Liv. Can we talk?"

"About what, Andrew? Are you about to be disrespectful and remind me that I can't give you a baby, which is the one thing that you want the most?"

Hearing my wife say that made me feel like shit.

"Nah, but you know what? Let's go to dinner. We can go to any restaurant you want."

She looked at me with a shocked expression on her face before saying, "Okay."

I grabbed my keys, and we headed out the door. We pulled up to Olive Garden about twenty minutes later. As soon as we were seated and ordered our drinks and food, I got straight to the point.

"Olivia, I just wanted to apologize for the way I've been treating you. I made you feel like less than a woman and started stepping out on you all because you can't have my baby. I know that shit has been rocky with us, but maybe we can go see a fertility doctor and see what the problem is."

"Andrew, what makes you think *I'm* the problem? Has it ever occurred to you that you may have a low sperm count?" she asked, catching me off guard.

She was right. I just assumed it was her and never thought for one minute that it was me.

"Honestly, I didn't think about that, but I'm

willing to do whatever it takes."

"Where is all this coming from? Just last night, I told you that you gave me something again, and you turned it on me, then left out and never came home. Now you want to work on us? It just feels sudden," she stated.

"I know this looks crazy, but when I left, I went to get a room, so I had some time to think about some shit. The one clear thing was that I didn't want to live life without you."

She took a few minutes to think it through before saying, "Okay, Andrew. I'm willing to try and work this out. It won't be easy for me, but I am willing to try."

And that was good enough for me.

Latrisha

Olivia has been calling me all day, and I've been ignoring her because I felt like shit for fucking her husband. The truth was, I hated how Andrew treated her and felt like she could do so much better than him. I knew it sounded crazy since I was fucking him, but I was serious when I told him I was through.

Andrew was a nice-looking man with hella swag and money. The problem was, he knew that and felt like he could do whatever he wanted to.

I wanted to tell my best friend so bad that I was

screwing her husband, but I couldn't afford to lose the closest person in my life.

I went to see my doctor yesterday and got tested. She still treated me as if I had it and told me she would call in a few days to let me know the results.

I'd just pulled up to Olivia's house. I was irked when I saw that Andrew was home. When I knocked on the door, Andrew answered and let me in.

"Babe, Trisha is here!" he yelled.

Olivia walked out of the bedroom and came into the living room.

"Hey, what's up with you? It feels like I haven't seen you in forever," she said.

I haven't seen Olivia since last week—since the day I was over here when she found out she had chlamydia. We texted every day, but I wasn't ready to face her yet.

"I know. I've been busy with work."

"Well, come in the room. I'm in here organizing my closet."

We walked into the room and sat on the bed.

"What's been going on with you?" I asked.

"Well, for starters, I got a teaching position at

Yorkship Elementary School. I start next week," she said excitedly.

My eyes widened with shock because I was surprised Andrew was okay with her working. "I'm so happy for you. I'm surprised that your husband is okay with you working."

"He doesn't know yet, but I plan to tell him later tonight over dinner. I don't care how he feels about it. I'm going to do this for me; I deserve it."

I couldn't lie. I was happy that she grew a pair of balls and did something for herself. However, he was going to flip out when she told him. He was adamant about her not working.

"I'm proud of you, bestie."

"Thank you."

For the next twenty minutes, she caught me up on what was going on with her and Andrew. I was surprised when she said that things were going well with them and how it was his idea to work on their marriage and go see a fertility doctor.

After we were caught up, I decided to head home. A part of me didn't want them to work out because she truly did deserve better. But who was I to judge when I was just as bad and slimy as he was?

When I walked out of the room to leave, Andrew

was in the kitchen cooking. I didn't even bother to look at him.

When I got in the house, I sat on my bed thinking about how everything got so fucked up.

The name is Latrisha Green, but all my friends called me Trisha or Trish. I'm thirty-five years old, and I was born and raised in Camden, New Jersey. I owned a planning event company. As a matter of fact, that was how I met Olivia and Andrew.

Olivia was so cool that we remained friends, even after their wedding. At the time, she and Andrew seemed like the perfect couple, and I was honored to help plan her wedding.

For some reason, I found myself sitting on the couch crying. I didn't know how I ended up betraying my best friend for some no-good nigga. I didn't know if I should tell her or take that shit to my grave. Either way, if she ever found out, that would be the end of our friendship.

My parents would be so disgusted with me if they knew what I did to my best friend. I thought back to two months ago, to the first time that Andrew and I had sex.

I was at a local bar, and I'd had one too many drinks. Andrew and one of his coworkers had just walked in to have a drink. At first, I was trying to hide from him because I didn't want him to see me. For the last year,

Andrew and I hadn't been seeing eye to eye because of how he started treating Olivia.

When I got up to use the bathroom, that was when he spotted me.

"Trish?"

"Oh, hey, Andrew," I slurred.

"Are you by yourself?" he asked.

"Yes."

"Well, I think you've had too many drinks to drive home, so I'm going to take you."

"I'm fine. I can drive myself home, thank you very much."

"Trish, that wasn't a question. Now get your things. I'm taking you home now."

I just rolled my eyes and grabbed my belongings. Andrew put me in his car and took me home. When we got to my house, he walked me in, and I started popping shit.

"Does my best friend know you're at the bar? I hate how you treat her. That's why I don't like you now," I slurred.

He just laughed at my comment.

"What's so damn funny?"

"Your ass is funny, Trish. The only reason you so-called 'don't like me' is because, deep down, you want me. You want this dick, don't you?" he said, closing into my personal space.

The next thing I knew, we were kissing. One thing led to another, and I had slept with Andrew.

The next morning, I thought that I was dreaming about what had taken place until I realized that I didn't have my car. I looked at my phone, and I had a text from Olivia telling me to call her when I woke up because she was going to bring me my car. I wondered if he had told her everything or not, but it was clear that he left out the part that we slept together.

Although it's been two months, we haven't slept together that many times. It was only four times. As much as I didn't like him, I hated that we had a sexual connection. Every time they got into it, he ran to me, and I was stupid enough to give in.

Shane

A nigga was fresh out of jail, and I needed some pussy like yesterday, so I was about to go get some from my daughter's mom. I had been cased for, like, three months on some bullshit charges that some hating ass cop was able to make stick.

I had a lawyer who talked a good game but wasn't about shit, so I had my right-hand man, which was also my best friend, Ricky, find me the best lawyer he could. Once he found me a good lawyer, I was out and ready to get back to business.

Money wasn't a thing for me and Ricky. Our money was long, and we were making some big moves that we decided to keep to ourselves.

I'd just pulled up to my baby mom's crib, and as soon as I walked into the house, my baby girl ran and jumped into my arms.

"Daddy! I missed you so much."

"Daddy missed you too, baby. More than anything."

Katrina walked out of the kitchen and was looking good as hell. I was contemplating if I wanted to fuck or not because every time I hit it, she started tripping and shit. I wasn't beat for all that shit, so I was good on her.

I was going to hit up this chick named Mariah I fucked with. As bad as I needed some pussy, I had to see my daughter first. I'd get some pussy later because my baby came before any bitch.

"Wassup, baby dad?" Katrina said with a big smile.

"Wassup, baby momma?"

"Not much. Layla, go play in your room so Mommy can talk to Daddy," she told my daughter. "Shane, I'm going to need more money for Layla. She's about to start school, which means she will need more things."

I looked at her ass like she was crazy because she had to be out of her damn mind talking to me like I was some dead beat.

"Katrina, I'm not sure if you're playing or not, but I'm not in the mood for your games right now."

"Shane, I'm not playing. I'm about to put your ass on child support," she said, pissing me off.

"Look, Katrina. I'm not going to keep going through this shit when it comes to my daughter. Every time you get your ass on your shoulders, you wanna start popping shit about putting me on child support. Yeah, my daughter lives with you, but I'm the one who takes care of her *and* your ass too, if we want to get technical. You didn't have shit when I met you. If you keep this shit up, I'll take my daughter to come live with me and then I'll put your stupid ass on child support, just to show you how it feels."

"Fuck you, Shane! Do you think a judge will ever give a drug-dealing thug like you a kid? *And* you just got out of jail!" she yelled.

"Katrina, we would never make it to the courts. You know not to fucking play with me when it comes to my daughter. That's an easy way for anyone to sign their death certificate, and that includes you. The next time you say some stupid ass shit like that to me, I'm taking my daughter."

Her ass got quiet because she knew I didn't play about my daughter. I didn't even know why she tried it.

"And you talking about I just got out of jail, but you and my daughter were well taken care of while I was in there. You have some fucking nerve," I told her.

I wasn't about to play with Katrina. I called my baby back downstairs and kissed her goodbye before leaving.

The name is Shane Hill. I'm twenty-four years old. I was born and raised in the streets of Camden. I'd been a street nigga since I could remember.

My best friend, Ricky, and I started our own drug set when we were fourteen years old. We always had the mindset of a boss. We always knew we didn't want to work for anyone.

We have mad money saved up, and we're working on getting out of the game. I had no intentions of being in this shit forever. After I had my daughter, I knew it was time to do better. I wanted more for my baby girl. I wanted her to be able to look up to me. Not to mention, I wanted to leave her something if something ever happened to me.

Katrina and I were just fucking around, and I slipped up and got her pregnant. At first, I wasn't too happy about it because that wasn't how I wanted to bring a baby into the world. She and I weren't even in a relationship, but I believed in kids having a two-parent home.

After Katrina decided that she was going to keep the baby, she and I tried to be in a relationship, but that shit wasn't working out. We'd be great co-parents until she got her ass on her shoulders and wanted to start her shit.

My daughter, Layla, was my heart. She was three years old and about to start preschool soon. It felt like she was just born, and now, in a couple of weeks, she would be starting school.

After I left Katrina's house, I went to meet up with Ricky. We had some business that we needed to handle. Ricky and I have been friends since the second grade. He was the brother I never had.

I had one younger sister, Shyann, who was twenty years old. I was protective over her, and I often acted as her dad instead of her brother, so you could only imagine how I acted when it came to my daughter.

"Yo, bro, wassup with you?" Ricky said when I walked up on his porch.

"Shit, just left from my crazy ass baby momma's house. She started talking that child support shit again before I told her that if she keeps fucking with me, I'll take Layla and let her live with me. That bitch had the nerve to say, 'What judge will give a drug-dealing thug like you a child?' But she shut the fuck up when I told her we would never make it into a courtroom and that I will take Layla and put her ass on child support."

"I told you when it comes to Katrina it's not Layla that she's arguing about. You should've known the bullshit was coming," Ricky said, then chuckled at his own comment.

"You don't think I know that? I'm a damn good father, and neither of them don't want for anything. If she didn't act so crazy every time I gave her the dick, I wouldn't mind hitting that whenever I wanted to get my dick wet. I just don't trust her when she starts talking about that child support shit, which is why I haven't told her I was going legit in a few months. I want to have one up on her in case she does try to take me to court. I will make her look so stupid when I present paperwork with our company's name on it."

"I'm glad I don't have those problems. I'm good with just having a Goddaughter for now. The woman who has my kids will be my wife. I love pussy, but not enough to nut in it," Ricky stated.

"I never thought I would have a kid right now, but now that I do, I couldn't picture my life without Layla. She's my world."

Me and Ricky decided to open up a car rental spot, and we've recently bought a few rental properties; some for tenants and some for vacation homes. We have always had a plan to get out of the game, so all the money we've saved up since we were fourteen came in handy.

Once we got everything off the ground and started making even more money, we would buy some more shit. Neither of us told anybody what we were doing; we just did it. Sometimes, telling too many people how you moving could bite you in the ass.

"Speaking of women, you still fucking with that Mariah chick?" Ricky asked.

"Just here and there. She's the only one I like fucking, so when I'm in the mood for some ass, I hit her up. I like her because she doesn't sweat me and lets me do me. We're both on the same page. But right now, I'm focused on making a better living for Layla."

"I feel you on that one. I want to be straight for my wife and kids, you feel me?"

"Hell yeah. That's where I'm at with it."

A lot of people thought because Ricky and I were young that we were like the rest of these young boys. Nah, me and my bro were different on every level. We wanted to be somebody. We wanted a wife and kids.

Me, personally, I wanted to settle down within the

next two years.

After we smoked a blunt, we went to meet up with the realtor we were buying the properties from. We had to sign a few pieces of paperwork and then everything would be official.

Olivia

I couldn't believe the first day of school was in two days. I had just finished setting up my classroom for the kids. Now all I had to do was write out their name tags for their tables and chairs.

As of right now, I have ten kids on the roster, but I was told I would more than likely get up to twenty to twenty-five kids. When I come in tomorrow, I'd do the bulletin board.

Things at home were going pretty good. Andrew was still always gone, but when he was home, we weren't arguing like we normally did. The last argument we had was when I told him about the job, but it was an argument he didn't win.

Since that night, he's been pretty cool. I wasn't sure what the big deal was anyway. He was hardly home with me, so being gone for eight hours a day wouldn't make a difference, one way or another. I guess that was just his way of being in control.

Once I was finished at work, I headed to the grocery store. I had a taste for some spaghetti tonight. As I was shopping, this young guy caught my attention. He was pushing who looked to be his daughter in the shopping cart.

"Daddy, can we please get some ice cream and chips?" the pretty little girl asked.

"Princess, you can have whatever you want. We're going to have so much fun this weekend. Tomorrow, we are going to see grandma and grandpa, then I have a big surprise for you," he said.

"Yayy, I love surprises!"

I got so caught up in seeing a father with his daughter I didn't realize I was staring until the young boy spoke.

"How you doing?"

"Hi, I'm sorry. I didn't mean to stare. I just think

it's so nice to see a man with their kid."

"No apology needed. The name is Shane, and this little one here is Layla," he said, holding out his hand for me to shake.

"Olivia." I shook his hand.

The little girl then waved at me, and I waved back.

"I see that you're married. Do you have kids?" he asked.

"Married, yes. Kids, no. Well, take care," I said as I walked down the aisle to get the rest of my ingredients.

"It was nice meeting you!" he called behind me.

I was so embarrassed he caught me staring at him. I was staring because I thought it was cute that he was with his daughter, but I was also staring because he was a nice-looking man. He gave me young thug vibes, but it was something about him.

After I paid for my groceries, I headed home. As soon as I got in the house, I put dinner on.

Andrew wouldn't be home until next week. He was in Atlanta drawing up some shit for this big Fortune Five Hundred company. I loved the fact that he made a great living for us, but I often felt alone most of the time.

Sometimes, it didn't feel like I was married. It felt like Andrew just came to visit from time to time. And it was obvious while he was away working, it was more than just his job he was working.

I wasn't sure why I dealt with Andrew and his cheating shit. He's never put his hands on me, but mentally, he made me feel like shit. Well, he did choke me once, and that was enough.

I guess I was scared that if my marriage didn't work, my mom would never let me forget about it. My parents didn't have a problem with Andrew, but they did feel like we got married too fast.

I didn't involve them in the shit that was going on between me and Andrew. They would have come to New Jersey and dragged me out of here themselves. My mom and dad moved to Atlanta two years ago. So whenever we talked, I pretended that everything was great in my marriage.

I called Trish to see if she wanted to keep me company, but she said she couldn't come because she had some work shit to handle. I wasn't sure what it was, but Trish has been acting a little weird for the last few months. I couldn't recall anything happening between the two of us, but something was off with her. I made a mental note holla' at her about it.

Once the food was done, I sat in the living room and watched *911* while I ate my spaghetti. For some reason, the guy, Shane, and his daughter crossed my mind. She was so pretty with long hair and light skin.

Nevertheless, Andrew and I went to the fertility doctor last week, and we both took a few tests. I was nervous to get the results because the last thing I wanted to hear was that I wasn't able to have children. I loved kids and would love nothing more than to have a few of my own. The doctor said that we should know something within the next couple of weeks.

After I ate and my show went off, I got in the shower and got my clothes out for work.

Latrisha

For the last few weeks, I've been sick as a dog. Shit hasn't been the greatest between Olivia and I, but that was on me. Although I haven't been with Andrew since just before we had words, the guilt was eating me up.

A few days ago, Olivia asked me to stop by her house because she needed to talk to me. I was so damn nervous, but when I got there, she wanted to know if she did anything wrong, which only made me feel like shit even more than I already did. Part of me wanted to tell her so bad about what I did because keeping this secret was killing me.

I haven't talked to Andrew since the night he left my house. I made up some lie about work to hide why I was so distant.

I had just finished making myself something to eat, and I was hungry as hell. As soon as I ate three spoonful's of my food, I had to throw up. I couldn't understand why I was throwing up. This was one of my favorite meals.

When I was finished puking my brains out, I thought about the last time I had my period. I didn't come on this month, which meant I was late. I jumped up and ran out the door and went to Walmart.

As soon as I got in Walmart, I went straight to where they kept the pregnancy test and grabbed about six of them. I rushed back to the house and took the first test. Minutes went by, and as clear as day, it read, *pregnant*. I wasn't beat for the answer, so I went and took another test, but it also said I was pregnant.

All I could do was cry. I started pacing the floor back and forth, cursing myself. I didn't know what to do. I was carrying my best friend's husband's baby, and to make matters worse, they didn't have any kids together.

This would crush Olivia.

I hated myself for what I did. I didn't believe in

abortions, but I might have to make an exception for this one. I couldn't even tell anybody or get any advice. I lay on the bed and cried myself to sleep.

***

It'd been two weeks since I found out I was pregnant. I went to the doctor a few days ago just to confirm it. I found out I was two months, and the pregnancy was taking a toll on me already.

I've been sick every day—just throwing up and sleeping. I could hardly work, and I damn sure couldn't go around Olivia because she would know something was up. A part of me was glad she had a job because that didn't leave her as much time as before.

I thought about if I should tell Andrew or not. I mean, he was the father, and he had the right to know. At the moment, he was the only person I could actually tell. And I needed to get this off my chest.

Me: *Hey, Andrew. I know it's been a while, but I really need you to come over today. We need to talk. It's important.*

A whole hour went by, and he still didn't text back. I was lying on the couch, and I heard my phone buzz. When I picked up the phone, it was Andrew.

Andrew: *Open the door. I'm outside.*

My heart was racing because I didn't have time to prepare myself. I thought he would have at least texted to let me know that he was on his way. As soon as I unlocked the door, Andrew walked in.

"Wassup, Trisha? What's so important that I had to come over here?" he asked as soon as he walked through the door.

"Look, there's no easy way to say this, so I'm just going to say it. I'm pregnant."

"What did you just say?"

"I said, I'm pregnant. I took a test two weeks ago, but I didn't want to say anything until I went to the doctor, which they confirmed a few days ago."

Before I knew it, the tears were running down my face. At first, he just stood there in silence, then he rubbed his hands down his face before he sat down on the couch.

"So are you telling me I'm going to be a daddy?" he asked, sounding a little too excited.

"What I'm saying is that I'm pregnant, but you know I can't keep this baby. What about Olivia?"

"We would have to deal with that when the time comes. But if you think I'm going to let you get rid of my baby, as bad as I want a child, you have another thing coming," he said.

"Andrew, she's your wife and my best friend."

"Look, I need to know. Are you sure it's my baby?"

"I'm positive. I haven't been with anyone else."

"Then I'm sure that you're keeping it. I'll deal with my wife when the time comes, but for now, just keep your mouth shut until I figure some shit out."

I just nodded my head in agreement. I couldn't believe what was happening.

Andrew didn't stay long, and I was left alone with my thoughts. This was insane. I couldn't keep this baby. I had to get rid of it and say that I had a miscarriage. I cursed myself for telling Andrew I was pregnant.

Olivia

It's been exactly one month since I've been a teacher, and I loved every moment of it. I have the most adorable class. I had twelve students so far, but was expected to get three more kids next week.

It was after school hours, and I was waiting to meet with the parents for Back-to-School night. I was excited to meet everyone and talk to them about their children. Plus, some of the things they could expect them to learn in my classroom, as well as the things from them as parents.

For the most part, I've met all of my students' parents—mainly the moms—a few of their fathers. Being as though they were the ones who had to sign their kids in and out of class, a few parents started to come in with their kids.

My eyes widened when the guy I met at the supermarket with his daughter walked in. I couldn't believe I didn't recognize the little girl. Crazily, she was one of my favorite students.

"Good afternoon, everyone. Most of you already know who I am, and for those who don't, my name is Mrs. Palmer. It's an honor to have your children in my class. I will not keep you long. I just wanted to tell you a few things about what your children will be learning in my class throughout the year, as well as what would be expected from you as parents.

"I know most people hear the word *preschool* and associate it with daycare, but your children will be learning. From their alphabet to numbers, days of the week, seasons of the year—as well as the twelve months in a year. I will also be teaching them basic math and sight words, weather, etc.

"The papers that you have in front of you are my information sheets. You can call, text, or email me at any time. I'm the teacher who will always be here for you and your kids, no matter the time. I would like to think of your children as my children. Does anyone have any questions? Okay, since there are no questions, let me show you some of the things your children have done so far."

I walked around the classroom and showed them their children's work. I kept feeling someone staring at me, and it was the young man from the supermarket. I was trying to stay focused and professional, but he was making me uncomfortable.

He was a young boy for sure, but he was damn sure fine. All the parents had left, except the young boy, who was still hanging around.

"Wow. I never thought I would see you again, just to find out your my daughter's teacher."

"Yeah, it's a small world. Layla is a joy to have in my class. She's a sweet girl with a huge personality."

"That's my baby. So I'm going to get right to the point. I've been thinking about you ever since I saw you at that market. I know you're married, but my question is, are you happily married?"

This young boy was seriously playing with me right now. I thought about what he asked. I knew I wasn't happy, but I couldn't tell him that, so I simply lied.

"Yes, I am. I'm very happy."

"Before you try to convince me, maybe you should convince yourself that you're happy," he said, then licked his lips.

I needed him to leave because this young man was sexy and charming, and I was married, lonely, and horny. And trust me when I tell you that shit didn't mix. Even though Andrew and I were somewhat in a better place, we haven't had sex because I still didn't trust him, and I wasn't that comfortable with him just yet to have sex with him.

"Listen, Mr., um…"

"The name is Mr. Hill, but my friends just call me Shane."

"Well, Mr. Hill, I need to get home. Again, it's a pleasure to have your daughter in my class."

"I'm glad she's in your class too. It gives me an excuse to come to see you," he said, licking his lips.

"If you don't mind me asking, how old are you?"

"I'm twenty-four, but I'll be twenty-five next month."

"Even if weren't married, you're way too young for me to date."

"Age ain't nothing but a number. Don't let the age fool you. I'm on my grown man shit," he said in a sexy tone.

I knew I needed to stop talking and take my ass

home to this empty house.

"I need to go," I told him.

"Before you go, just take my number and only call me if you need anything. Or when you realize that you're married to the wrong man," he asserted, taking it upon himself to put his number in my phone.

As bad as I wanted to stop him, a part of me was glad he put his number in my phone. Shane finally left, and I was relieved because I was uncomfortable. It was something about him that made me feel warm inside.

***

Andrew thought I went to Atlanta to see my parents, but I decided not to go. Shit has been feeling a little weird with him lately, so I wanted to see what he would do if he thought I was in another state.

I stayed at the hotel last night, but I decided to come home and see what he was up to. I've been trying to call Andrew to see when he was going to get back, but as usual, he didn't answer.

When I pulled up to my house, I was confused as to why I saw Andrew's and Trisha's car parked out front. I got out of the car and walked onto the porch. For some reason, I had the weirdest feeling take over my body.

I eased the key in the door, and when I opened the door, no one was in the living room. I tiptoed into my room and damn near had a heart attack when I saw my husband and my best friend in my fucking bed sleeping peacefully.

The rage, hurt, and anger that took over my body was unreal. I could only get one of them, so I choose her. I walked around to the side of the bed where she was sleeping peacefully.

I beat her ass out of the bed. She started screaming when she saw what was going on. I was swinging and yelling while never missing a punch. Trish was begging me to stop, while Andrew tried to pull me off of her. I kicked her in the stomach, and Andrew started yelling.

"Olivia, stop, she's pregnant!" he yelled, now gaining my full attention.

The feeling that came upon me was like something I've never felt before in my life.

"What the fuck did you just say!" I yelled, now charging at Andrew with full force.

I swear it felt like I was a superhero in this bitch because I was moving fast and swinging even faster. These two had me fucked up. I knew some shit was off, but I wasn't expecting any shit like this. She was the same bitch in my ear about how I deserved better. I guess those rules didn't apply to her trifling ass.

"Olivia, you need to calm down! You're acting like a crazy person!"

"Fuck you, Andrew! You're fucking my so-called 'best friend,' in my fucking house, in bed my bed, and then gonna say she's pregnant, yet *I'm* the one acting crazy? I should kill both of y'all!" I yelled before throwing a lamp at him.

Someone knocked on the door.

"Police, open up!" I heard the officer say.

I slowly walked over and opened the door.

"Good morning. We got a disturbance call. Is everything okay?"

"Well, let's see. I come home to catch my husband and my best friend in my bed, so no, I'm not alright," I said while laughing like a crazy woman.

The officer walked in and looked around the house. "Is everyone okay?"

Both of them nodded their heads.

He looked over at Trisha and saw that she was bleeding. "Ma'am, are you okay? Do you want to press charges?"

"Officer, I'm fine. I just want to get my belongings and leave," she cried.

The officer took all of our statements and advised Andrew to leave for a few days. He waited for Trisha to get her shit and leave, and my soon-to-be ex-husband did the same.

Once everyone was gone, I sat on the couch and looked around at the mess I caused in here. I was finally coming down from the adrenaline rush, and the reality of what just happened started to kick in.

I sat there rocking back and forth, not knowing how to feel. I didn't have anyone to talk to. I lost my husband and my best friend. I felt lost, confused, and betrayed. I knew Andrew wasn't faithful, but how could he fuck with my best friend? Out of all the people in the world, they choose each other. I found myself sitting on the couch, crying my heart out.

***

It was the next day, and it still felt like a dream. But the mess that was made yesterday during the chaos reminded me that it was real. All I wanted to do was sleep the day away, so I didn't have to face this horrible reality.

I got up to use the bathroom, then came back to the couch and cried myself back to sleep.

My phone going off caused me to wake up. I looked at the phone, and it was a text message from an unknown number.

Unknown: *Hi, beautiful. This is Shane. I know that this may be totally inappropriate, but I can't seem to get you off my mind. I got your information off the contact form you gave out.*

I read the text twice before deciding to respond.

Me: *Hello. You're right, this is inappropriate, but what's done is done, so what can I do for you?*

Unknown: *I would love to take you out on a date. I know you're married, and you're my daughter's teacher, but I would really love to get to know you better.*

I knew that I shouldn't go out with him, but I was lonely and hurting and could use some company. I didn't have any friends outside of Trisha. I had some family, but I wasn't prepared to answer questions that I wasn't ready to address just yet. At least if I talked to him, I could tell him what I wanted him to know.

Me: *You can meet me at Long Horn Steak House in*

Cherry Hill at 6 p.m.

Unknown: *Yes. Thanks for giving me a chance.*

Me: *I will see you tonight.*

I knew he thought I was doing this for him, but it was honestly for me. I didn't want to lead him on and make him think we could be something because that could never happen. He was a baby in my eyes. I had damn near eleven years on him. Not to mention that I'm his daughter's teacher.

It was 4:30 p.m., and I still haven't showered yet. I was dreading going into the bedroom Andrew and I once shared, but I had no other choice because I needed some clothes.

After showering and getting dressed, I looked in the mirror so I could do my hair and instantly regretted agreeing to go out with Shane. My eyes were so swollen and puffy, and I didn't want him to see me like this, but I wasn't the one to go back on my word. Also, I needed to eat. Although I wasn't hungry, I haven't eaten anything since yesterday.

I pulled up to the restaurant at ten minutes to five. I got out the car and walked into the building. Shane was already here and seated. I walked over to the table, and he got up and pulled out my chair.

That was sweet of him. I couldn't remember the last time Andrew and I have even been out together.

"Thank you."

"No thanks needed."

After we put in our drink order, Shane stared intensely at me for a moment. He was about to say something until the waiter came back with our drinks.

"I know this question may be none of my business, but are you okay? Your eyes are red and puffy like you've been crying."

I knew I should have kept my ass home. "I honestly don't want to talk about it. So let's just order our food."

"Your wish is my command," he said with his hands in the air.

After we ordered our food, the more we talked, the more comfortable I became with him.

"So why did you agree to come out with me tonight?" he asked, catching me off guard.

I thought about if I wanted to open up or even if I should. If he was a complete stranger, I would have probably put all my business on the table. I was feeling like crap and needed someone to talk to, but him being my student's father was what made me hesitate.

"Honestly, I needed a distraction, and I needed to get out of the house."

He just nodded his headed and stared at me for a moment before he spoke. "I take it your husband pissed you off?"

"Look, I'm not comfortable talking to you about my personal life, especially since you're the father of one of my students. But if you must know, I caught my husband with my best friend. And in the midst of me beating her ass, he yelled that she was pregnant. I've never felt so disrespected and hurt in my life. So, yeah, that's why it looks like I've been crying because that's all I've been doing since yesterday," I told him honestly.

A tear fell from my eyes, and I hated that I was crying in front of this young boy. I felt weak and was now ready to go home and cry myself back to sleep.

Shane didn't say anything. He got up and moved his chair directly next to mine and grabbed my hand. "Oliva, I'm sorry that happened to you, and I know it's gonna be hard to get that memory and betrayal out of your mind, but anybody who could do some foul shit to the person they vowed to love and cherish for life, with a person who was supposed to be your ride or die, doesn't deserve your tears.

"What they do deserve is to see you walking away with your head up high and moving on with a boss nigga like me. What they did to you will eat them alive, and they will be miserable for the rest of their low lives. I don't know you that good as of yet, and I hope what I'm about to say isn't too forward.

"I've wanted you since the first day I laid eyes on you, and since he fucked up, that allows me the opportunity to make you mine. To make love to every single inch of your body. And before you respond, I know you're not ready to move forward just yet, because you need time to heal, but I'll wait for as long as it takes you to get that nigga completely out of your system. Because when I make you mine, I need your heart, body, and soul to be completely available for only me."

My mouth was a little dry, but my pussy was wet and throbbing on the chair. This young boy had balls speaking to me like that. I knew we could never be, but it felt good—so good to feel wanted and desired by a man.

The last time I had sex was almost two months ago with my husband, and he gave me an STD. So I was due for some dick. However, I didn't respond to what he said because I didn't know what to say.

"Thanks for tonight. I needed this," I told him.

"I don't want you to be alone tonight. You can come to my crib, and I swear, I won't do anything you don't want me to do. You can even sleep in my guest room if you're not comfortable. You shouldn't be alone right now or in that house. I'm sure you're not ready to face him yet," he said, rubbing the back of my hand.

I knew he was right about me being alone. I just didn't think being with him was the greatest idea either.

"I don't think would be a good idea."

"Tell me why it's not a good idea. Look, I know you don't know me and that you don't trust me yet, but just know that I'm not going to harm you. Let me take care of you and help you get through this heartbreak."

For the first time in a long time, I was going to do something I wanted to do. Although I didn't know him well, he was a sweetheart, and I didn't want to be alone.

"Okay, I can do that," I said above a whisper. "But no funny business."

"I promise I'll be on my best behavior," he said,

smiling.

Shane was a handsome young man. He had a perfectly brown complexion with light brown eyes and an awarding winning smile with two deep dimples. His waves were deep and thick too.

After he paid for the food, he left a tip, then we walked out of the restaurant. Shane walked me to my car and opened the door. When I got in, he closed the door and leaned into the window.

"Do you need to go home and grab an overnight back?"

"I do need something to put on, but I don't want to go home right now, so I'll just go by Walmart."

"A'ight, cool. Follow me to my house, then we can drive to Walmart together."

Andrew

After getting in from the hospital with Trisha, I went home, but I didn't see Olivia's car when I pulled up. When I walked into the house, it was still torn up.

I went and packed some shit up as fast as I could. I grabbed my work stuff from the office and some clothes and my laptop. I put my things in the car and went to grab a few more items. After I put the last few things in the car, I headed to my best friend, Joey's, house. I pulled up to Joey's house because I needed someone to talk to. I knocked on the door, and he answered wearing some baller shorts and a wife-beater.

"Damn, nigga, you look like shit. Are you good?" he said as soon as I walked in the door.

"Nah, I'm not okay. I fucked up pretty bad this time. I think I lost Olivia for good," I told him while shaking my head. "She caught me with Trisha in our bed," I admitted.

Joey's eyes got wide. "Nigga, I know damn well you're not talking about her best friend?"

"Yup, that's not even the worst part of it. Trisha's pregnant."

"You have lost your damn mind, Andrew. When did you become this guy? When did shit with you and Olivia get so bad? It's not bad enough that you fucked around on your wife, so you did it with her best friend and got her pregnant?"

"Look, I don't know how shit got this far, but I didn't come here to be judged. I just need a friend."

"I wouldn't be a friend if I didn't tell you that this is fucked up. I love you, but you deserve everything thing that happens from here on out. You get your wife's best friend pregnant? As good as Olivia is to you? If I had a woman like Olivia, it wouldn't be a woman in the world to make me cheat on her."

It was something about the way he was talking

about my wife that was pissing me off. It made me wonder if he had a thing for my wife. I came to the wrong place. I cut the conversation short and left. I hopped in the car and pulled up to the Aloft hotel.

***

It's been two weeks since that shit went down with me and Oliva, and she still hasn't said a word to me. Every time I called her phone, it went straight to voicemail, and she changed the locks.

I knew she was upset, but that was my house too. I didn't want to get the authorities involved, but I planned to go to the house, and if she didn't let me in, then I would have to do what I had to do.

I pulled up to the house, and her car was parked out front. I went and knocked on the door. I felt like a damn fool knocking on my own door.

"Who is it?" Olivia answered.

"It's me, Andrew."

Surprisingly, she opened up the door, and man, she looked so fucking good. I just wanted to rip her clothes off. She stepped to the side and let me in.

"Hey, Oliva. You look nice."

"That's nothing new, Andrew. That's obviously

why you married me. It had to be for my looks because it damn sure wasn't for any of that shit you said in those fake ass vows you stated to me in front of God and all of our family and friends."

"I didn't come here for all this, Olivia."

"And I didn't ask to be married to a lying, cheating, backstabbing bastard. So I guess we can't always get what we want, now can we?" Olivia said, then sat on the couch.

I knew that she was hot with me, but Olivia has never been this damn mouthy. I wasn't sure if I could get used to her being this way.

"While you're here, please humor me and tell me what you want?"

"I don't want to fight with you, but this is my house too, and I'm not going to stay in hotels when I have a home."

"I don't have a problem with you staying in your home. You can stay in the room and sleep in the bed that you shared with that tramp ass hoe. I already moved out of the room that we once shared. I will never step foot in that room again," she said, walking off to a different part of the house.

I didn't bother to say anything because I made my bed, so I guess I had to lay in it. I walked into the room, and memories of that day replayed in my head.

I hated myself for what I did, and it was my fault for telling Trisha to come over.

The crazy thing was, we didn't even fuck. She wasn't feeling good, and I told her to come over so I could keep an eye on her. I should have just let her sleep in one of the guest rooms or went to her house. I thought Oliva was in Atlanta visiting her parents.

I haven't talked to Trisha since the day I dropped her off from the hospital. I didn't feel like being bothered with her right now. I had to find a way to work shit out with my wife. I couldn't imagine my life with her.

Shane

I was in the car waiting for Ricky. We were on our way to sign the final paperwork for our real estate business, then we would be doing the same for the dealership, and we'd officially be business owners. This would be our last week in the game because we had to get everything up and running.

"Yo, bro, wassup? Are you ready to officially become a businessman?" Ricky asked when he got in the car?

"Nigga, we been businessmen, but now we're

about to become legit. We finally made it out of the game, bro. We've been blessed with no record, and we're both still alive. Most dudes our age that's in the game are either locked up or dead."

"Hell yeah. Anyway, what you been up to?"

"Not much. I have just been chilling with Olivia."

"You talking about Layla's teacher?"

"Yes, I'm feeling her. I just wish her ass wasn't married, but she cool as shit. Not to mention, she already loves my daughter."

"Just be careful, bro. She's a married woman, and she's also broken. You sound like you're feeling her, but you know she may never get over that hurt. Just be careful, bro."

I didn't respond, but I knew he was right. I wasn't sure how she felt about me because this was a lot for her to process. I just wanted her to be good. She was too beautiful of a woman to be looking sad and hurt all the time. I could tell she didn't hang with too many people, so I knew that shit made it even harder.

After we signed our paperwork, the two of us went out for drinks to celebrate. After we left the bar, I dropped Ricky back off at home, then took my ass home. When I got in the house, I stripped out of my clothes and took a shower, then lay on the bed and grabbed my phone so I could call Olivia.

"Hello?" her sweet voice answered.

"Hello, beautiful. How are you feeling?"

"I'm pretty good today. I just finished grading some papers. I'm about to take a hot bubble bath and have a glass of wine."

"I wish I was that bathwater."

I could tell that she was smiling. But I was dead ass serious. The thought of her with no clothes on sitting in the water had my dick hard as hell. It's been a minute since I had some pussy.

"You're so crazy. How was your day?"

"My day was great. I would like to see you tomorrow. I want to show you something. I'll make you some dinner," I told her.

She agreed to come over, and after talking for a little longer, I hung the phone. I thought back to the night that she spent the night at my house. It was crazy how she and I connected so well. We stayed up most of the night, just talking and getting to know each other. Every time I was around her, my dick got rock hard.

I think I might have to call up Mariah. It's been a minute since I called her up. I shot Mariah a text.

Me: *Hey, ma. Wassup with you? Can I slide through?*

Mariah: *Hey, love. Yes, I just got out of the shower, so hit me up when you're on the way.*

Me: *I'm on my way now. Just have the door unlocked, and don't have any clothes on. I want you to start playing with the pussy when you think I'm close by.*

Mariah: *Okay, Daddy.*

I smiled at her text, then put on some sweats and a t-shirt. I didn't plan on doing any talking when I got there, just straight fucking.

As soon as I walked into the house, I locked the door and headed to her bedroom. Just before I opened the door, I heard moaning and knew she was doing what I told her to do.

I walked into the room and climbed on the bed. I removed her fingers, placed her arms over her head, and started playing with her pussy. I started eating her pussy like it was my last meal. Mariah grabbed my head, and I stopped.

"Keep your fucking hands up there," I told her before continuing to feast on her pussy.

After making her cum, I got up and took my

clothes off. I slid on a condom and went to work. I swear it seemed like we were fucking for hours. After we both nutted, we lay on the bed in silence for a minute. Mariah reached over on her nightstand and grabbed a blunt. After she took a few puffs, she passed it to me. I hit that shit and just lay there.

"I'm so glad that you hit me up. I was horny as hell," she said, passing me the blunt.

"Tell me about it. I been a little busy, so fucking wasn't my priority."

"Same here." After we finished smoking, I got up, used the bathroom, and put my clothes on. I sat on the bed next to Mariah. "I'm about to go, ma,'" I told her, placing a kiss on her cheek.

"Okay, Daddy. Until next time," she said.

I got up and walked out the door, making sure to lock it.

I fucked with Mariah the long way. She didn't run her mouth, she never bitched about what we had, and not once has she hit me with the "What are we?" question. we never talked about anything personal, just basic shit and fucking. I always came to her house because I didn't allow women over to my crib. I surprised myself when I let Olivia come over.

***

"Daddy!" Layla yelled when I walked into her classroom.

"Hey, baby girl. Mommy asked me to pick you up, so we're going to hang out for a little bit," I told her.

While she got her belongings, I walked over to talk to Olivia. She was looking extra good for some reason today. She had on a black pencil skirt, an indigo blue shirt, and some blue pumps. Her hair hung past her shoulders, and I wanted to throw her on the desk and eat her pussy. Just beautiful.

"Hey, Liv. You look extra beautiful today."

"Hey, Shane. Thank you," she said with a smile.

I couldn't afford to have a hard dick in the middle of a preschool class.

"I'm surprised to see you here today."

"Katrina asked me to pick her up today because she's working late. I'm going to take her to see my mom for a bit before I drop her off. Dinner should be done around eight p.m.," I told her.

"Okay, I'll see you tonight. Have fun."

"Bye, Mrs. Palmer. I'll see you Monday," Layla said.

"Bye, sweetheart," Olivia said.

I strapped my baby girl in the car and pulled off. The entire ride to my mom's crib, all I could think about was Olivia. I was trying to be patient, but I wanted her to divorce that piece of shit husband of hers, so I could show her how a woman should be treated. I knew I said I would wait, but the more we talked and spent time together, it only made me want her more.

I pulled up to my mom's crib, which was located in the Parkside area of Camden. I knocked on the door instead of using my key. My mom was a tad bit on the wild side, and you could catch her fucking in the living on the floor. I couldn't afford to traumatize my little girl like that.

My mom answered the door, and a wide smile appeared on her face when she saw that it was Layla and I at the door.

"Hey, baby. This is a surprise to see you today. What brings you by?" she asked, picking up and carrying her into the house.

My mom was my everything. Sometimes, we came off as brother and sister; that was how close we were. Don't get it fucked up, though. My mom would fuck me up if I ever crossed the line and disrespected her in any way.

"I picked Layla up for Katrina, and I figured that I would bring her over to see you this weekend since I have plans with her next weekend."

"Well, I'm glad that you came over. I'm always in the mood to see my favorite people."

After my mom gave Layla a snack, Layla went up to her room. My daughter was spoiled and had her own fully-decorated room over here, at my house, at her house, and at Ricky's house. The crazy thing was, Layla has never spent the night at Ricky's house. The only time she went in the room was if we stopped by and we needed to discuss some business.

I sat down at the kitchen counter and talked with my mom as she cooked her dinner.

"So, son, what's going on with you?"

"I've just been busy, Mom. Trying to make this money so that you, my daughter, and wife, when I get one, are well taken care of," I told her.

"Shane, I keep telling you that we will be good. It's time for you to get out of these streets so you can be alive for all of us."

"I'm glad that you said that because I have something to show you."

I walked to my car to grab a folder. When I came back, I handed it to her. She opened the folder and read the papers, then looked up at me with confusion written over her face.

"Baby, what is this?"

"Ricky and I are legit. We're out the game," I told her, smiling. "We own not one, but two businesses. We finalized everything earlier."

"Oh my God, I'm so proud of you, baby. Now momma can sleep better at night knowing that you're not out here in these streets. I'm so proud of you and Ricky." My mom hugged me so tight and kissed me on my cheek. "I love you so much, Shane."

"I love you too, Mom."

It felt so good to see that smile on her face. After chilling with my moms for a little longer, I dropped Layla off at home, and I still had to go home and cook. I was glad that today was Friday, so Olivia didn't have to work in the morning, because dinner was going to be a little late.

Olivia

I was at work finishing up with some paperwork. I had been staying later than I normally stayed because I had no reason to rush home.

I planned to take a trip to see my parents this weekend. I planned to leave as soon as school was over. Friday was a half-day, and there was no school on Monday, so that worked out. I would normally go down there with Andrew or Trisha, but that wasn't happening.

Andrew kept trying to have small talk, but I was

done with his ass. I either ignored him altogether, or popped shit. I was waiting for him to be served with divorce papers any day now. I should have been left his sorry ass. I wasn't sure what happened to the man I married, but I wasn't going to stick around any longer to find out.

I've been hanging out with Shane here and there, but we spoke daily. Although Shane was eleven years younger than I, he was so mature. I was starting to like Shane more than I should have, and him leaving the streets and going legit made me like him even more.

I wasn't sure if Shane was spitting game or being nice because he wanted some ass, but he made me feel all bubbly inside whenever I was in his presence. Or even on the phone with him. I swear, he said all the right things at the right times. He was the one who helped me realize I deserved so much more than Andrew.

"Really, Olivia? You had me served with fucking divorce papers?" I heard Andrew's voice yelling.

I looked up at him like he was crazy because this nigga had the balls to pop up to my place of business.

"Andrew, you are unbelievable. How dare you bring this mess to my job?"

"So it's that easy for you to divorce me? No conversation or nothing?"

"Andrew, we were done talking the minute you fucked my best friend and got her pregnant. What did you think would happen? Did you think we would be one big happy family? What, did you expect me to be your child's Godmom and stepmom? I need you to leave, and leave now."

"I'm not going anywhere until we talk."

Before I could respond, I heard a voice.

"Olivia, are you okay?"

I looked up, and it was Shane. This was bad. I needed to deescalate this situation quickly before things went left, someone got hurt, and I lost my job. I wasn't even sure what Shane was doing here because Layla wasn't here, so I was confused.

"Yes, I'm fine. Is everything okay? I wasn't expecting to see you," I asked.

"Yo, who the fuck are you? And my wife's well-being isn't any of your damn business," Andrew said.

Shane walked up and stood in front of Andrew. "Listen, I don't do well with disrespect, and who I am isn't important. She asked you to leave, so I think you should leave. This is your wife's place of business. Don't you care if she loses her job?" Shane asked, looking Andrew directly in his eyes, not showing an ounce of fear.

"Look, you little punk. I suggest you mind your business and get the hell out of here. This has nothing to do with you."

"Call me another punk, and I'm going to show you how much of a punk I'm not," Shane said. His face was tight, and I could see the anger in his eyes.

"Shane, I'm okay, and I'm sorry that you had to walk into this mess of mine."

"No apology needed. I came to pick up Layla's book back and lunchbox. Her mom asked me to come grab it, and I'm glad I did."

"It's in her cubby. I didn't realize that she had left it."

"Thanks a lot. Are you're going to be good here with this guy?"

I put on a smile and nodded. "Yes, I'll be okay. Also there's a permission slip in her folder to the Pumpkin Farm."

"Okay, have a good night," he said while starring at Andrew.

As soon as Shane left, the smile disappeared off my face. Before I could say anything, Andrew had his hands wrapped around my throat.

"So you going to stand in my face and disrespect me like I ain't shit!"

I wasn't sure where security came from, but I was glad they showed up. Andrew had truly lost his damn mind, and he was going to pay. I just prayed I didn't lose my job behind this.

"Are you okay, Mrs. Palmer?" one of the security guards asked.

"Yes, I am, thanks to you."

They escorted Andrew out of the building, and I stayed behind because I was going to wait for the police to get here.

"I'm going to go back up to the front desk. I'll send the officers to the class, and don't worry, he won't be back."

I gave him a thankful nod. "Thank you so much."

"No thanks needed. This is my job."

When he walked out of the room, I sat at my desk. I could feel the tears forming in my eyes. I couldn't believe how bad my marriage took a turn for the worst in just one year. I would have never imagined my marriage ending in a divorce.

Before our baby problems happened, the two of us were inseparable. I never had to worry about feeling alone because Andrew was so attentive to my every need. He made sure that I never wanted for anything. Not mentally, physically, sexually, or financially. But

I guess that having a baby was just that important to him.

The crazy thing was, the fertility doctor called me with the results right after I found about Andrew and Trisha, and nothing was wrong with either of us. Nothing showed up that indicated that we couldn't have kids.

"Hello, are you Mrs. Palmer?" an officer asked.

"Yes, I am."

I told the officers what happened, and after I told them everything, I went down to the station to press charges. I hated that things had to be this way, but I was tired of dealing with his abuse and disrespect.

My parents would lose their shit if they knew how Andrew has been treating me. Since Mr. Andrew couldn't keep his hands to himself, I filed for a restraining order. I knew that one of us would have to leave the house, so I decided to go to the house with a police escort to grabbed and much as I could fit in my truck. I wasn't too worried because I had plenty of money saved up.

Although I was a housewife and didn't plan for my marriage to end in divorce, I knew I had to be smart and put money away. My momma raised no fool. Now I just had to find a hotel that I wanted to stay in until I could find another place to live.

I decided on the DoubleTree hotel in Mt Laurel. I paid up for two weeks. Hopefully, I could find something within that time. After I got settled, I ordered room service, then lay on the bed to see what was on TV.

I lay there on the bed going over today's events, and I couldn't believe that Andrew came up to my job and choked me because I filed for a divorce. I heard a knock on my door, and I knew it was room service. I opened the door to get my food. As soon as I was done eating, my phone rang. I picked it up, and it was Shane.

"Hello?" I answered.

"Hey, beautiful. Are you good?"

I contemplated if I should tell him what happened or not. "Honestly, I don't know. As soon as you left out the room, Andrew choked me, but security came immediately, so I wasn't hurt."

The line went silent for a moment. "What the fuck you mean, that nigga chocked you?"

"Calm down, Shane. I called the cops and pressed charges, and I filed for a restraining order."

"That shit ain't cool. I'm not okay with that pussy touching you. He's going to pay."

"Shane, please let me handle him. I don't need you

to fight my battles, although it's nice to know that you have my back."

Shane didn't respond to my comment. Instead, he changed the subject.

"We're you at now, ma?"

"I checked into the DoubleTree hotel. I'm going to stay here until I find myself a spot. I paid up for two weeks. Hopefully, I get something by then, but if not, I'll just pay for another two weeks. I want a spot within a month, though. I don't want to be associated with the house I once shared with Andrew."

"You could have stayed at my house in the guest room instead of wasting money, but let's link tonight."

"Thanks for the offer, but I need to work through this on my own, and I just want to stay in tonight. Tomorrow after work, I plan to go to Atlanta to see my parents. I'll be back sometime Monday so I can get ready for work."

"A'ight, ma. Do you tonight. I know you probably need some alone time, but if you need me, you know where to find me."

"Thanks, Shaney, I said not realizing I had given him a nickname"

"Shaney, huh? Well, you have a good night, and

Liv. Remember, no crying over him," he said, giving me a nickname as well.

"Good night, Shane."

With that, we disconnected the call. I lay back on the bed and thought about how sweet Shane was. Before I knew it, I had dozed off.

***

The next day at work, I was on my lunch break in the break room when I heard my name being paged on the loudspeaker. All I could think about was losing my job. My stomach was doing backflips as I made my way to the main office.

When I walked into the office, the receptionist told me that the principal wanted to speak to me. I walked into her office, and she looked up at me and spoke.

"Good morning, Mrs. Palmer. I heard about yesterday, and I just wanted to make sure that you were okay. Should I make sure that he doesn't come back?"

"Good afternoon. I'm sorry that happened. It won't happen again, and yes, I'm okay. I'm going through a divorce, so he was upset. I filed for a restraining order, so if he shows up, I don't want to see him."

"I'm glad that you're okay, and okay, I'll let the

office and security know."

"Thank you so much." I looked on the desk and noticed the beautiful red and white bouquet of flowers. "Those are some beautiful flowers," I told her.

"I'm glad that you like them because they just came for you," she said with a smile as she handed me the flowers.

A look of confusion appeared on my face when she said they were for me. I didn't want to read the card in front of her, so I simply said thank you and headed out of the office. I was sure that the flowers were from my sorry ass husband, but if he thought some flowers would make up for the shit he put me through, he had another thing coming.

I walked back to the class and sat the flowers on the desk. The kids were still outside, so I sat down and read the card.

I just wanted you to know that I was thinking about you. You're beautiful in every aspect of the world. I hope you feel better today than you did yesterday. I'm sorry that you're going through so much. I hope these roses will put a smile on your face and make you feel better. Much love, Shane.

I was smiling so hard that my face was beginning to hurt. This man was unbelievable.

Me: *Thank you for the roses. They're beautiful. You have no idea how much I appreciate these flowers. It means a lot. I owe you.*

Shane: *I'm glad that you liked the flowers, and you don't owe me anything. But I do have a favor to ask. My birthday is coming up in two weeks, and I'm having a small gathering. I would love nothing more than for you to be my date.*

I read the text twice, and I still didn't know what to say. I wasn't ready to be seen in public with a man, especially a young one at that. This was something I had to think about.

Me: *Shane, that is sweet of you, but I don't know if I'm ready for all that just yet. I'm not saying no just yet, but I do need to think about it. The kids are on their way in from lunch, so I'll talk to you when I get settled in Atlanta.*

Shane: *Okay, have a safe trip. It's no pressure about the party, but it would really make my birthday a great one.*

I smiled at Shane's text and put my phone away.

After my workday, I headed straight to the airport. It was time to get away from Jersey and go see my parents.

Almost two hours later, I was finally in Atlanta. I rented a car, then went straight to my parents' house. When I got there, I knocked on the door. My dad opened the door, and I hugged him tightly.

"Hey, baby girl. I'm so happy to see you. It seems like forever since I've seen you."

"I missed you too, Daddy. Where's Mom?"

"Olivia, baby, you look great. Go wash up. You're just in time for dinner. I made some of your favorites."

After sharing a hug with my mom, I went upstairs and used the bathroom. I grabbed a washcloth and washed my hands and face. By the time I got downstairs, there was a spread on the table, and I couldn't wait because I was starving and couldn't remember the last I had a homecooked meal.

When I sat down, my dad say grace and began to eat. We had ribs, chicken, fish, baked mac and cheese, collard greens, and cornbread. And even though it wasn't on the table, I knew that there was some type of cake. My parents owned a catering company and could both throw down in the kitchen, so this food was good as hell.

"So where's that husband of yours? I'm not used to you coming alone. Usually, if you don't come with him, you usually come with Trisha," my mom asked.

I was prepared for this conversation, and I was ready to get it over with because this would be the last time I would have to tell this story until we started the divorce proceedings start. My lawyer said it shouldn't take that long unless Andrew tries to make things difficult, which I was sure he would.

"Well, there is no easy way to this, so I'm just going to say it. I'm divorcing Andrew. For the last year, we've been trying to have a baby. And because it was taking too long to happen, he thought that by cheating on me and treating me like crap was okay."

"Oh my God, I'm so sorry, hunny. Why haven't you said anything before now?" my dad asked.

"I was trying to be a wife and fight for my marriage, but all of that went out the window a few weeks ago when I walked in on him in Trisha in my bed. I dragged her out the bed while I was beating her down, just to be hit with an even bigger blow to the gut when Andrew yelled that she was pregnant," I told them while taking a bite of my rib.

"What the hell did you just say, Olivia? Because I thought I heard you say that your best friend was pregnant by your husband?" my mom asked with her mouth hanging open.

"Well, then, you heard right. Yes, I'm hurt and lost a best friend, but I've realized my worth, and I'm ready to be free and move on. I honestly don't want to talk about it anymore."

"I'm so sorry, baby girl. We had no idea you were going through that. Did he put his hands on you?" my dad asked.

"He's chocked me a couple of times, but most of his abuse was mental. I just pressed charges a few days ago and filed a restraining order. He came to my job and choked me because he was served with the divorce papers."

My dad's face was red and tight, which was why I left that part out, but once he asked, I couldn't lie.

"I'm going to kill that piece of shit," my dad said angrily.

"Dad, I know you're upset, but I can handle this."

"No one put's their hands on my little girl and gets away with it. Now this conversation is over," he said, getting up from the table.

The rest of the night was silent and awkward. I could tell that my mom wanted to inquire more but decided to respect my wishes.

Once my parents went up to bed, I decided to go up and get some rest as well. After my shower, I texted Shane, and he ended up calling me. He and I talked until a little after 2 a.m. I loved talking to him.

He always made me feel better. When we hung up, I fell asleep right away. I slept like a baby, which was a first since everything went down.

Andrew

"Man, my life is falling apart. I can't believe she's divorcing me. We haven't had one conversation since she caught me, and just like, that it's over?" I said to Joey.

The two of us were at work sitting in my office, talking about my marriage.

"Look, I know that you're probably going to be pissed at what I'm about to say, but as your best friend, I would feel like shit if I don't say it." I looked over at him, not sure that I wanted to hear what he had to say.

"Just say what you need to say."

"Drew, you had a great fucking woman, and you fucked around on her numerous times within the last year all because she couldn't get pregnant. Not once did you check to see what the problem was, or if she was the problem. You went bed-hopping. Not to mention, you were neglecting her. Olivia still worked through it like the good wife she was, but nope. That wasn't good enough for your ass. You went and did the unthinkable and fucked her best friend got her pregnant.

"Please tell me what's there to talk about? How would you feel if I fucked Olivia and got her pregnant? Giving her the one thing that you couldn't. Are you telling me that you would stay with her and still be my best friend? You fucked up badly, and now, you have to deal with the consequences. Now, you have your baby with no wife to share it with. So stop bitching every day like she's the one doing something wrong. This is all on you, bro."

Joey's words cut me deep as hell, and I was so busy having my head stuck up my ass that I never even thought about it that way. There was only one way to even try to get my wife back, and that was to convince Trisha to get an abortion. I had to decide which one I wanted more: a baby or my wife? Before I could respond, there was a knock on my door.

Joey answered the door, and in walked two officers.

"We're looking for an Andrew Palmer?"

"That's me. May I ask what this is about?"

"We have a warrant for your arrest for the assault of Olivia Palmer."

The cops placed my hands behind my back and read me my rights. I couldn't believe I was being arrested. I never thought in a million years that she would press charges on me. I guess she was truly sick of my shit.

A few hours later, I was out of jail, thanks to Joey for bailing me out. This was becoming too much for me to handle.

"Nigga, what the fuck is going on? What are they talking about, assault?"

"I went up to Olivia's job when I found out about the divorce filing, and I choked her and was escorted out by security," I told.

"Okay, Andrew, you're losing your fucking mind. You better chill the fuck out before you lose more than just your wife; you're going to lose your freedom. You need to fix this shit. I hope that bitch was worth all of this. She better have the best pussy ever."

I just shook my head because he was right. I was losing my fucking head. He took me back to my job, so I could get my car. The ride back was quiet. The entire time, all I could do was think. I knew I had to make some major changes. I decided to take a few personal days so I could get a lawyer and talk to Latrisha and figure out how we were going to deal with this.

***

I just pulled up to Trisha's house. It was time for us to talk. I haven't talked to her since I dropped her off from the hospital. I rang the bell, and she opened the door. She had a small baby bump, and I couldn't believe that I had a baby on the way.

"Hey," she spoke a little above a whisper.

"Hey, Trisha. I think we need to talk. What are we going to do about the baby?"

She looked at me like I had two heads. "What exactly do you mean? It's too late to abort. I'm a little over three months now, so we're going to have a baby. I don't expect for us to be together or even be friends. I just need you to be there for your child. I don't need you to be at the appointments and bring me over food. I know that what it is."

I just put my hands on my head because I created a mess.

"Look, we created a mess, and this bay didn't ask to be here, so I'll be there every step of the way. I already lost my wife, so I have nothing else to lose. Just let me know if you need anything, and keep me up to date with the appointments. I'll come to as many as possible. Have you talked to Olivia at all?"

"Not since the day she beat my ass. I miss her like crazy, but I think this is it for us, and I don't blame her. The truth is, I don't know how to face her. I know we will never be friends again, but I at least want to talk to her and apologize."

"I'm sorry for being selfish and breaking up y'all friendship. We both lost something great for a nut. Now she's divorcing me."

"Wow, I feel like shit. I can hardly look at myself in the mirror. She was the only friend I had, and I betrayed her."

I talked to Trish for a little longer before leaving and going to my empty home.

Latrisha

I was in Walmart picking up a few items, and out of the corner of my eye, I could have sworn I saw Olivia. I walked down the next aisle, and there she was. I haven't seen her since that day she caught me at the house.

"Olivia?" I called out.

She turned around and looked at me with a look of disgust. "You have some fucking nerve to call my name like we're friends. If I could beat your ass again without going to jail, I would beat the shit out of you."

"Olivia, please hear me out. I know that I fucked up, but please just talk to me," I pleaded.

She laughed in my face loudly, catching me off guard and making a scene. "Everyone, do see hear this pregnant woman right here? Well, guess what? She's carrying my husband's baby, and the worst part is, she was my best friend! she yelled.

People started whispering and pulling out their phones to record. I couldn't have been more embarrassed.

"Olivia, I know you're hurt, but please don't this."

"Fuck you, Trisha. You're a fucking fake and a phony. What kind of woman plans their best friend's wedding, then fucks her husband and gets pregnant by him? And you don't think this is necessary? You don't want everyone to know who you really are?" she asked, walking closer to me. "You're dead to me. Don't call me, don't text me, and if you ever see me out and about, do yourself a favor and turn the other way because if you don't, I *will* beat your ass," she threatened before walking off.

Leaving my cart right in the aisle, I ran out of the store and straight to my car. All I could do was cry my heart out.

Seeing Olivia for the first time in damn near a

month made me miss her even more, but I also knew the two of us were done after the way she spoke to me. If I wasn't sure before, I was sure when I saw the pain and anger in her eyes.

I finally stop crying and took my ass home. I was sure that this shit was going to be all over the internet. When I got home, I took my ass to sleep because this shit was just too much to handle.

I knew that Andrew wanted to keep this baby, but I wasn't too sure that was the greatest idea. The damage was done, but I didn't have to add fuel to the fire. I didn't even like Andrew like that. We slipped up, and the dick ended up being good, but good dick wasn't going to help me raise a child.

***

I was at the Cherry Hill Women's center about to get an abortion. I decided that keeping this baby was the best choice for me. I didn't have my best friend, and everyone was now looking at me sideways, so I was thinking about moving away and starting over.

My cousin, Tina, was here with me.

"So what are you going to do when he starts asking questions about the pregnancy?"

"I haven't thought that far out yet. I just knew that I wasn't ready to tell him just yet. I'm thinking about moving away, and if I do, I'll leave him a note telling him what I did."

"Damn, cuz. This shit is crazy, but I'm still going to be here for you. Just know I will never leave my man alone with you."

My cousin hurt my feelings, but I guess I couldn't blame her. A few minutes later, I was called to the back for my procedure.

My cousin dropped me off at home once I was finished, and I slept for the rest of the day. I woke up from my nap a little sore. I used the bathroom, then went to find something quick to eat. As soon as I was finished eating, I took my ass back to sleep. Maybe when I woke up in the morning, I'd feel better about myself. Because I felt worse now than I did before I got rid of the baby.

Shane

"Damn, bro, I was wondering when you were going to make it down here to see me," my little sister, Shyann, said when I walked up.

"My bad, sis. Ever since I got out, I've been busy as hell. I don't know if mom told you yet, but me and Ricky went legit. We did it big, and we have two businesses."

"Yeah, she told me. I'm proud of you, bro, and I haven't seen Ricky's sexy ass in a minute."

"Shyann, doesn't fucking play with me," I warned.

"Boy, bye. It's not my fault that your best friend is sexy as hell."

I have only been here for ten minutes, and my sister was already doing my head in.

"Anyway, you know a nigga's birthday is this Friday, and I'm having a little get together. It wouldn't be complete if my baby sister wasn't there."

"Oh, shit! You came here to personally invite me? I feel special," she teased.

"That's cool. I was planning to come home for the weekend anyway. I figured something would be going down for the big day."

Shyann was in college for business, and she attended Howard University in DC.

"Cool. If you don't have class on Thursday, I'll come to scoop you then, so I'm not driving back and forth on Friday. I need the entire day to get fresh to death and shut shit down, unless Mommy picks you up."

"I don't have any Friday classes, and I only have one class on Thursday in the morning, but I'll be done with that class at eleven. So I'll be ready when you get here."

"A'ight, bet. That sounds good. I should get here by noon. Let's go grab something eat. I'm hungry as hell."

The two of us went to grab some food before I headed back to Jersey. On the ride home, I thought about how beautiful my sister grew up to be. I had a few years on her, but she and I were close. I paid for her to go to school so she could do something with her life and not be out here fucking with these lames.

I couldn't wait to talk to Olivia later today to see how things went with her lame ass husband. Today, the two of them, along with their lawyers, were having their first meeting. I didn't care what happened with that nigga. I had something planned for his.

I wasn't feeling him putting his hands on Olivia. He's a pussy for that one. I despised that nigga and her best friend, and I didn't know either of them. I've been watching his bitch ass, so I could make my move when the time was right. I might've gotten out of the game, but I was still a thug at heart and would still kill a nigga. And he was the first on my list.

I hoped like hell that Olivia would be my date for my birthday, but I didn't think she was going to be comfortable with it.

I made it back home, and I was tired as shit from all that driving. So I took my ass to sleep. I had a long day tomorrow.

***

The next day when I woke up, the I jumped into the shower and got dressed. I decided on some blue jeans and a wheat-colored sweater with a pair of Timberlands.

I was heading over to meet with the contractors for the houses I had. I was having a few things done to each property. It was nothing major, just some minor things to make the place pop a little more. I knew once everything was complete, we were going to make a killing. Between the car rentals and the properties, our families would be set for life. We'd decided that if anything was to happen to us that we would split the properties in half.

Ricky was meeting up with an event planner today to go over the details for the party on Friday. I couldn't believe I was turning twenty-five already. But it felt good to know that my family was set because of me. I always had a hustler's mentality. I heard I got it from my dad.

My dad died when my mom was pregnant with my sister, so I guess I was about four at the time. Shyann never got to meet him, but I do remember him vaguely. My mom said he died, but I think my dad was killed. I truly believed he was in the game because when I first started selling drugs, she would always tell me that I was just like my father, and if I kept going the way I was going, that I would end up just like him.

While I was waiting for the contractor, I decided to shoot Olivia a text.

Me: *Good morning, beautiful. How are you this morning?*

Olivia: *Good morning. I'm pretty good. How are you?*

Me: *Great, now that I talked to you. I wanted to know if you have given any more thought to coming to my party and being my date?*

Olivia: *I'm flattered, but I don't think that I'm going to go. But if I change my mind, I'll let you know.*

Her text put a damper on my day, and I hoped she would change her mind, but I wasn't going to bring it up again. I was feeling Olivia, but the one thing I didn't do was beg for a woman's time and presence. I typically only asked one time and one time only, but because of her circumstances, I was trying to be patient.

Me: *A'ight cool enjoy the rest of your day.*

Olivia: *You too.*

I couldn't front and say that I wasn't feeling some type of way. I knew I was probably being petty, but I was going to fall back until figured out what the hell she wanted to do. I have been chilling when it came to getting my dick wet because I wanted to see how shit played out with us.

Once I was done with the contractors, I decided to hit up the mall. I still needed something to wear to my party. I had to make sure I looked good. I went over in my head if I wanted to tell Katrina about the party or not. The last thing I wanted was for my party to get fucked up. I just wanted to enjoy myself and my success.

Olivia

I had finished texting with Shane, and I could tell by his last response that he wasn't too happy with my answer. I just had a lot going on, and even though he was a sweet guy, I just wasn't ready to move on just yet.

It has only been a little over a month since everything went down. I was still staying in the hotel because I haven't found exactly what I was looking for yet. And when I moved, I wanted to be there for a while. I wanted to find something away from Andrew and Oliva but still close enough to my job.

I'd just walked into my lawyer's office for our second meeting. I was ready to be done with this divorce. When I got there, surprisingly, Andrew and his lawyer were already there. I hated to see his face, but I had no choice to see him. Every time I looked at him, a flashback popped into my head about the day I caught him with Trisha.

"Good morning. My client has decided to give you half of all assets, and he would also like to know if he can speak freely?" Andrew's lawyer said.

I thought about if I wanted to hear him or not. At first, I was about to object, but I decided to hear him out, and I felt like I needed to get some shit off my chest as well.

"I'm okay with that. Can you give us the room, please?" I asked.

Our lawyers looked at Andrew, and he gave them a nod. Our lawyers left the room, and as soon as the door closed, Andrew started to speak.

"Olivia, I know somewhere in our marriage I lost my way. I don't know why, but what I do know is, you didn't do anything. I fucked up in the worst way, and there is nothing I can say or do to change that. But I need you to know you are a great woman. I couldn't have asked for a better wife.

"I don't want you to leave this marriage questioning yourself because you were perfect. I'm sorry for everything I've put you through. I'm not going to object to anything that you asked for because you deserve that and more. And I know that you don't want to hear this, but I feel like I should tell you anyway.

"The shit that went down with me and Trisha should have never happened. I fucked up, and that was my fault as well. The first time it happened was the night that I told you that I took her home because she was too drunk to drive."

I looked over at him with my face ripped up because I remember that day like it was nothing. I even took her car to her house.

"Wow," was I could muster up to say.

The entire time he was talking, the tears were forming in my eyes, but after his last statement, they freely fell down my face.

"Olivia, I'm sorry, and I know that you're hurt, but she didn't want to sleep with me. That was on me too. She was actually cursing me out just before it went down. I know that what I'm saying won't make you feel any better, but I would hate to be the reason you lost a good friend."

I swear I wanted to get up and smack the hell out of him because he was pissing me off.

"Andrew, I spent the last year of our marriage

feeling like shit, feeling like less of a woman because of the way you treated me, all because I didn't get pregnant in a timely fashion. Well, now you don't have to worry about me getting pregnant because you got what you wanted. I just wish you didn't have to have a baby with the woman I thought was my best friend.

"I don't have much more to say. I wish you the best because thanks to you, for showing me that I deserved so much more, I'm going to live my best life, and that doesn't include you. And when we leave here, you will be a free man to do what you please, even more than you already were," I told him as I waved for the lawyers to come back in the room.

Once the lawyers came in, I wiped my face and held my head high. I was done with this marriage, and Andrew. I sat there and signed away my marriage, and I was feeling good about it. I walked out of the office feeling like the bad bitch I was. I had one more stop to make before I left, so I could be completely done with this situation.

I pulled up to Trisha's house, and I was glad to see she was home because I wanted to get this over with this today. I needed to move on. I knocked on the door, and Trisha opened the door. When she saw that it was me, she looked like she saw a ghost.

"Look, I'm not going to hit you or anything. I just came to get a few things off my chest, so I can move on. What you did was fucked up and a stab in the back, but I'm glad that I know who you really are. And don't worry. My ex-husband explained that he was the one who came on to you when you were drunk, but how I see it is, you wanted it because if you didn't, you wouldn't have kept doing it.

"If you would've told me then, I may have been able to forgive you, but now I'm done. I just wanted to tell you that I wish you and your baby the best. As long as I continue to be bitter, I can't move on, but you were right about one thing. *I do* deserve better than Andrew, but you deserve a man like him. I wish y'all the best. Goodbye," I told her, walking off the porch, not giving her a chance to respond.

Before I made it to the car, I heard her yell out, "Olivia, I got an abortion!"

I didn't bother to respond. I got in my car and drove off. I now had $1.5 million dollars in the bank, and a house. It was the house that we once shared, but I didn't want to live there anymore, so I might just sell it or rent it out. My next stop was the phone store. It was a must that I changed my number. The first person that I called was Shane.

"Hello?" he answered.

"Hey, Shane. It's Liv. I just wanted to let you know that I changed my number, so lock it in."

"A'ight. Wassup with you?"

"Not much. Are you busy?"

"Nah, I'm just chilling."

"Would you like to join me at Texas roadhouse? I'm starving and could use some of those good rolls."

"Hell yeah. Drive to my house, and I'll drive."

"Okay. I'll be there in about ten minutes."

I was smiling the entire ride to Shane's. I wasn't sure what came over me, but I was looking at life in a different light. I felt free, and I enjoyed hanging out with Shane, so why shouldn't I? I wasn't sure about no relationship, but who said I couldn't see what the dick was about?

When I pulled up to Shane's, he was already warming up the car. When he saw me walk up, he got out of the car and hugged me before opening my door. Before getting into the car, something came over me, and I leaned in and placed a quick kiss on his lips. He looked at me with a surprised look but didn't say anything. He just smiled, which made me smile.

When we got to the restaurant, I ordered the catfish with a baked potato and corn, and he ordered steak, a baked potato, and corn.

I could feel him staring at me, so I looked up at him, and he just looked me in the eyes.

"You seem different. What did I miss?" he asked,

grabbing my hand.

"Honestly, I'm ready to live again. It's been a while since I felt free. And if I could be honest, most of the thanks goes to you. You helped me realize my worth, and for that, I thank you," I told him honestly.

Shane thought the world of me before really getting to know me, and the more time we spent together and talked, he consistently reminded me of who should be. And for that, I would forever be so grateful.

"No thanks needed. I just see something in you. I know I haven't known you that long, but I know you were special the first day I saw you in the market. I don't take you becoming Layla's teacher by accident. I believe that God put us together he placed us in each other's lives for a reason.

"I'm not sure what that means, but I know that I like you and like having you in my life. As bad as I would love to make you mine, right here and now, I know you're not ready. All I can do is respect that and your decision. If it's meant, then we will be. But for now, let's toast for a new friendship."

We raised our glasses and made a toast.

"To friends," I said before taking a drink. "Shane, if you would still have me, I would be honored to be your date for your party."

"Of course, I will still have you. Who else but you?"

After fighting with him to let me pay the bill, I finally won, and we headed back to his place. I got in my car and headed home. The truth was, I didn't trust myself with him alone tonight.

When I got back to the hotel room, I lay in bed playing back on today's events, and the only thing that stuck out was that quick kiss I planted on Shane's lips. They were so soft and had me curious if he was a good kisser or not.

I reached over and grabbed my little bullet that I bought last week and indulged in some self-love while fantasizing about Shane.

Shyann

I'd just gotten to Jersey from school. I decided to surprise my family and come a day earlier. That way, my brother wouldn't have to drive to come and get me. Plus, I wanted to catch the train.

When I got to the train station, I got a Lyft to my mom's crib. I knocked on the door, and my mom opened the door, surprised when she it was me.

"Shyann, what are you doing here? I thought that Shane was picking you up tomorrow?"

"I decided to surprise y'all and catch the train and come today. I'll be here for about two weeks."

"Is everything okay? Why are you staying so long? Won't you be missing out on school?"

"Mom, stop worrying. Everything is fine. I'm not missing anything. I'll be back home in a month anyway. It's graduation time, and you know I plan to come home to work."

"I was just making sure. Give me a hug."

I hugged my mom tightly. After we shared a hug, I walked into the kitchen.

"Please tell me that you cooked because I'm starving."

"Sorry, baby. I didn't cook, but let me call your brother and see if he wants to go out to dinner tonight. I don't normally cook dinner unless I'm having something or company. If I would have known that you were coming, I would have cooked."

I went upstairs to put my bags in my room. When I walked into the room, it still looked exactly the way I felt it. I sat my stuff down and lay on my bed. I guess I must've been tired because before I knew it, I was asleep.

***

I woke up to a knock on the door.

"Come in!" I yelled.

My brother walked in the door and jumped on the bed like a big kid. "Why didn't you tell me that you were coming home?"

"It's called a surprise. Now let's go eat because I'm starving."

We walked downstairs, and the first face I saw was Ricky's fine ass. I swear that nigga could get the pussy whenever he wanted it.

"Hey, Ricky," I spoke when I got downstairs.

"What's up, big head?" he said, pulling me in for a hug. "I haven't seen you in a minute."

He smelled so good that I didn't want to let him go. I broke the hug and just stared at him.

"I know, right? It's been a minute."

The four of us went out to dinner, and I couldn't do shit but think about Ricky. I knew Ricky would never fuck with me because of my age, but most importantly, he would never break his loyalty to my brother.

My brother would never let me be with Ricky. Why? I don't know. I wasn't a little girl anymore. I've had a crush on Ricky my entire life but knew I could never act on it.

Ricky was practically raised with us. He and Shane were so busy in the street life that when his parents moved, he didn't want to go with them, so he stayed with us. He would have been like a brother except I always had a crush on him.

After we ate, we all left. When I got back to the house, I sat in the living room and talked to my mom for a bit.

"Shyann, you know it will never happen, right?" my mom asked, breaking me from my thoughts.

I had no idea what the hell she was even talking about.

"Mom, what will never happen?"

"You and Ricky," she said with a smile.

"Mom, I have no clue what you're talking about."

"I saw you eye-fucking him all night. Your brother would have a heart attack if y'all messed around. Besides, I practically raised that boy."

"Mom, ain't nobody checking for that boy. Anyway, thanks for dinner, but I'll see you in the morning. I'm so tired."

"Yeah, okay, Shyann, but goodnight. I'll see you in the morning."

"Goodnight, Mom," I said and walked up the

steps.

I had no idea that my crush for Ricky was so visible.

I took my ass to bed. That train ride had me tired, and dinner gave me the itis. Plus, I had an interview tomorrow for an office position that I wanted to check out. They were aware that I couldn't start for a few weeks, so If everything went well, I would be employed right after school. I wasn't planning to tell my family until I had the job.

***

The next morning, as soon as I woke up, I could smell the aroma of food, so I knew that my mom was cooking breakfast. I decided to shower and get dressed before heading downstairs.

My interview at Palmer's Enterprise was at eleven, and it was already a little after nine. Once I was dressed, I headed downstairs. I found my mom in the kitchen.

"Good morning, Mom."

"Good morning, Shyann. Where the hell are you going dressed like you're on our way to handle some business?"

"I just wanted to look fly today, but I do have

plans with Bree (my best friend) in a little bit. I should be home by dinner. I have to go to the mall and grab something for the party."

"Yeah, I need to get something to wear myself."

My mom and I talked while we ate breakfast.

Bree was right on time. She got there as soon as I was finished eating. I rushed out the door and got in the car with Bree.

"Hey, bitch. You look cute. I like that pants suit."

"Thanks, boo."

I was rocking a burgundy pants suit with a white blouse and some heeled boots. I had my hair in a high ponytail. Burgundy complemented my yellow complexion.

We pulled up to the job, and she said she would wait for me in the car. I got out of the car and walked into the building like the boss bitch I was. I had many different characters, and I used whatever one was required for the situation. I could be calm and etiquette or hood and rachet. And most of all, a boss bitch, and that was the character I wanted to use for this job interview.

When I walked in, I was amazed at the beautiful décor. This place was well thought out, and I loved it. I walked up to the receptionist and told her that I was here for the interview. She told me to have a seat and that Mr. Palmer would be with me shortly. I took my seat, and a few moments later, an office door opened and the good-looking man called me to the back. I couldn't lie. He was an older man, but he was fine as hell.

"Good morning, Ms. Hill," he greeted.

"Good morning, Mr. Palmer," I said, shaking his hand.

The entire time of the interview, all I could think about was if I got hired, how I wouldn't mind being on his desk getting fucked.

"Ms. Hill," I heard him call out.

I needed to get my shit together before I blew this interview.

"I'm sorry Mr. Palmer," I went into a daze for a moment.

"It's okay. It happens to the best of us. I just wanted to make sure that you were aware of what the job entitles if I were to give you the position?"

"Yes, I'm aware. I did my homework on the office and the job title before applying. I would be honored to work here, and feel like I would be a great asset if you hire me."

"How so?" he asked, then licked his lips.

"For starters, I have a big personality that could easily land you the clients you need and want. Not to mention, I am dedicated to any and everything that I do. Trust me, Mr. Palmer, you want me on your payroll, and I promise that you won't regret it."

He didn't say anything at first. He just rubbed his hands down his face before speaking. "I like your confidence; you wear it well. Although you will be starting a little later than I would like, I wouldn't want to interfere with your schooling, but I'm going to take a chance on you, Ms. Hill."

"I appreciate the opportunity to work here. I won't let you down. I just have a few more weeks, then I'll be here. My graduation is on a Thursday, so I can start fresh on Monday morning. I can start any trainings or meetings virtually until I'm home, if that's an option. I will email you my schedule."

"I like your way of thinking. I look forward to receiving your email."

I stood, and he did the same as he handed me a folder.

"After you fill out the paperwork, you can fax it back over to me. It was a pleasure talking to you."

"Thank you. It was a pleasure talking to you as well. Again, thanks for hiring me. I'll see you soon." I shook his hand and walked away.

I could feel that he was watching me walk away, so I put a little extra into my walk. I walked out of the building like the bad bitch I was, and when I got to Bree's car, I started dancing before I got in the car.

"Bitch, I got the job!" I yelled.

"Yes, bitch, I knew you would get it!" Bree said.

"Girl, my boss is fine as shit. I may have to fuck that nigga and give him some of this young pussy."

"Well, about how old is he?"

"I don't know. He's older than our asses, that's for sure. Maybe mid-thirties, I guess."

"Damn, bitch, that's old. You know damn well Shane would have that nigga's head if that old dude tried to talk to you."

"Shane is not my daddy, so Shane is the least of my worries. Now let's go to the mall to get something to wear for the party."

"I need the sexiest outfit I can find, and I hope that fine-ass brother of yours will finally notice me," Bree said, pulling off.

"Girl, I keep telling you that my brother isn't beat for no chicks right now. He's too busy trying to chase his paper and take care of my niece."

"I just want to fuck. I swear that nigga looks like

he has a big dick, and I'm almost certain that he knows what to do with it."

"Eww, I don't want to hear about my brother's dick, Bree."

We both laughed and as we pulled up to the mall.

Andrew

It'd been a long few weeks, so I decided to go out for a drink with Joey. Between the divorce, work shit, and having a baby coming, shit has been stressful.

We sat at the bar, and I ordered a Henny and Coke. As I was sipping my drink, I looked around the bar and spotted Trisha. I knew I had to be tripping because not only was she here, she was drinking.

"I'll be right back. Apparently, my baby mom has lost her damn mind. She's in here drinking like she's not pregnant with my fucking kid." I got up and walked over to the table that Trisha was sitting at. "Trisha, what the fuck are you doing at the bar?" I asked, voice laced with anger.

"Obviously, the same thing that you're doing here: drinking," she answered with a slur.

"Trisha, I'm not about to fucking play games in here with you. Get your ass up; you're going the fuck home."

"Fuck you, Andrew. You're not my fucking daddy, so get the fuck away from my table."

I swear I was losing my fucking patience with this girl. I took a deep breath, and I guess by my demeanor, Joey could tell that I wasn't happy, so he walked over to the table.

"Drew, are you good?" he asked.

"Nah, she in here drinking while she carrying my seed, then got a nerve to be in here talking shit."

Trisha started laughing like a crazy woman, now gaining the attention of everyone who was in the bar.

"Oh, that's right. You do still think that I'm carrying your child. I got rid of that damn baby. What the hell do I look like having your baby? You're my best friend's husband, Andrew!" she yelled.

Something took over me after processing what she said, and I smacked the shit out of her. Joey grabbed me, and she stood there holding her face.

"I can't believe you fucking hit me! I hate you, Andrew! You ruined my fucking life! I lost the most important person to me because you just had to stick your dick in me! I hate you!" she yelled. Trisha's outburst turned into her crying with her head down on the table.

"You wanna play the fucking victim? I lost my fucking wife over you because you said you were keeping the baby! Then you go behind my back and kill my seed without saying a word to me about it? That was fucked up, so you know what? Fuck you too!"

Joey took me outside to cool off and to get some air. That bitch had ruined my night, so I decided to leave. I've been staying with Joey while I was having my house built. Although I had more money than I knew what to do with, I always loved living in Gloucester city, but I decided to have a house built in Vorhees closer to my job. I had no reason to stay there anymore. I needed a fresh start.

I lay across the bed and thought about how my life changed so quickly. I was once happily married until I became an asshole and lost the best thing that ever happened to me. I was miserable without Olivia. I could hardly eat or sleep, and I thought about her all day, every day.

And it didn't help that whenever I talked about it with Joey, he made sure to remind me that it was my fault and that I was an asshole for throwing away my marriage with Olivia. Now I didn't bother to discuss how I was feeling with him. I knew he was just trying to be a great friend, but he wasn't helping me.

I lay in the bed, and the girl I interviewed crossed my mind. She was a beautiful girl. The problem was, she was too damn young, but it was something about her that I liked a lot. Apart of me wished I didn't hire her because I knew it would only be a matter of time before I had her ass sprawled out on my desk.

I was a very sexual man, but with everything being all fucked up, I haven't had any ass in a minute. I could tell she had a thing for me as well, but I wasn't into fucking around with no young girls. I was thirty-eight years old, and she was only twenty.

I heard a tap on the door and knew it was Joey.

"Come in."

"Yo, man, are you okay?" he asked, sitting in the chair across from the bed.

I didn't feel like hearing the "I told you so's" that Joey liked to give out, so I debated if I should speak freely.

"Look, Joey. I'm not okay, but I don't like talking to you about it because every time I tell you what I'm going through, instead of you being there as a friend and just having my back, you make me feel like shit. I don't need a reminder that I fucked up my marriage. I'm living in my shit every day. I went from having a home and a wife to sleeping at my best friend's house."

"You're right, and I didn't realize that's what I was doing, but you can talk to me about any and everything."

"I'm not okay, Joey. I can't sleep or eat, and all I want is a second chance with Olivia to get it right this time. I lost my wife because I fucked around with her best friend and got her pregnant. Just for Trisha to get an abortion. If she was going to do that, I could have saved my marriage. Now I lost everything over a baby that I'm not even having."

"Have you tried reaching out to Olivia to talk to her?"

"Nah, I know Olivia, and she's done. I lost her bro," I told him honestly.

I knew when Olivia got fed up with my shit that I would lose her for good. I just thought I had more time to get my shit together so it didn't come down to this.

"Damn, bro, I'm sorry. The only advice I have is to accept the fact that you lost her and move forward. I'm not telling you to jump back out there because I don't think your heart is ready. Maybe take a vacation and get away from all of this.

"I know it doesn't feel like it right now, but you will be just fine. Everything happens for a reason, so just let this be. If it's meant for you and Olivia, it will happen when the time is right."

"Yeah, I know. I'll figure it out. Well, I'm going to bed. I have a long day tomorrow."

"A'ight, bro. Try to get some sleep."

When Joey left out the room, I stripped out of my clothes and beat my shit while fantasizing over Ms. Hill.

Olivia

Tonight was Shane's party, and I was feeling nervous. Maybe even a little foolish for agreeing to attend this party. I was trying my best to live a little more and stop overthinking everything. Yeah, I had ten years on him, but it wasn't like I was marrying him and having his kid.

I was just about to finish getting dressed so I could go to the hair salon and get my hair done. I wanted something new and different; I wanted a new look. I walked into the salon and was greeted by who I assumed was the owner.

"Good morning. Welcome to Breanne's."

"Good morning. I have an appointment with Breanne."

"That would be me. Are you Olivia?"

"Yes, I am."

"Great. What would you like today?"

"Honestly, I have no clue. I just want a new look, but I need it to be fire."

The stylist looked and me and nodded her head. A smile appeared on her face as the perfect hairstyle popped into her head. "I have the perfect color and hairstyle for you."

She sent me over to the shampoo girl so I could get my hair washed. After my wash, I sat down in the chair, and Breanna started working her magic.

"Before I go too crazy, how much of this hair do you want to keep?"

I gave it some thought but realized I didn't care about hair at all.

"It's just hair, so do you. Just don't make me bald," I told her, and we both chuckled.

"Nah, you won't be bald at all. I'm going to give you some hair instead of taking some off."

I wasn't sure what the hell that meant, but I just went with the flow; that was what I've been on lately.

A little over an hour later, she was finally finished. She handed me the mirror, and when I looked in the mirror, I couldn't believe this was me. This hairstyle was everything. My hair was tapered down on one side with the prettiest bouncy curls. I now had autumn-colored hair that complimented my complexion perfectly. I couldn't wait for Shane to see me tonight.

"Wow, I love it! This is beautiful."

"I'm glad you like it. I think you look good with this hairstyle; it fits your complexion and your face."

"Thank you, and I agree. Well, I have to get out of here. I have a party to attend in a few hours."

"I know what you mean. I have an event to attend to myself. You're my last client."

I paid and made sure to give her a hefty tip. I knew from this day forth, I would be coming to her to get my hair done.

"Have a good day, and just so you know, you now have a new client from here on out."

"That's nice to hear. I'm glad you like it."

Before going back to the hotel, I stopped by the hair store to grab some large rollers. When I got into my suite, I rolled my hair up and took off my clothes, just leaving on my bra and panties.

I wanted something to eat so, I decided to order a bacon cheeseburger and fries. I heard my phone ring, and I knew that it was either my parents or Shane because they were the only ones with my new number.

"Hello?" I answered, using my sexy voice.

"Hey, beautiful. What you up to?"

"Not much. Just ordered a burger and fries. I'm starving. How's your birthday so far?"

"It's a'ight. I just been running around all day. I just can't wait until tonight so I can chill and have a little fun. But if I can be honest, the main part I'm looking forward to is seeing you tonight," he said, causing me to smile.

"If I can be honest, I can't wait to see you tonight either."

"I'm glad to hear that, beautiful. I'll be there to pick you up at 7 p.m., sharp."

"Okay, I'll be ready. Also, since I didn't get to do anything for you today, I would like to at least take you out to dinner or something."

"I would love that. How about I give you the entire day tomorrow? I don't have any plans, so if you want, we can chill all day. Why don't you pack an overnight bag, and you can spend the night? You can sleep in the room that you slept in when you stayed over before."

"I think I'd like that."

The two of us hung up, and I couldn't help but smile. I'd just thought of the perfect gift to give to Shane tonight. I think that it was time to see what that dick do.

I heard the door and knew it was my food. After I ate, I packed my bag and then showered. Once I was lotioned, I did my makeup. It's been so long since I dressed up and went out, so I was kind of excited.

It was now 6:45, and I knew Shane would be here any minute. I looked in the mirror and couldn't believe how sexy I looked. I had on a royal blue dress with a high split that was trimmed in silver rhinestones. I was rocking a pair of silver heels with rhinestones. Everything was perfect, and if the night went well, I would be getting some dick.

I heard a knock on my door.

"Just a minute," I said as I grabbed the rest of my things.

I knew that it was Shane.

When I opened the door, both of our eyes locked,

then we took each other's attire in, and I swear I could feel the juices dripping onto my panty line.

"Wow, you look like something out of a magazine," he said, twirling me around.

"You're looking good yourself, birthday boy," I told him.

Before I knew it, Shane leaned in and kissed me. I deepened the kiss and made myself even more hornier than I already was. I broke the kiss because I knew if I didn't, I would have never made it out of this room.

"Damn, Olivia. Don't start no shit you can't finish. You gotta nigga hard as hell. I'll leave all of those niggas at the party by themselves if I get to spend the night with you," he said, licking his lips.

"My bad, Shane. I shouldn't have done that. I just got caught in the moment."

"No apologies needed. I like the moment we're having. But let's get out of here before I stop being a gentleman."

We left out of the room because lawd knows if we didn't, neither of us would have made it to his party.

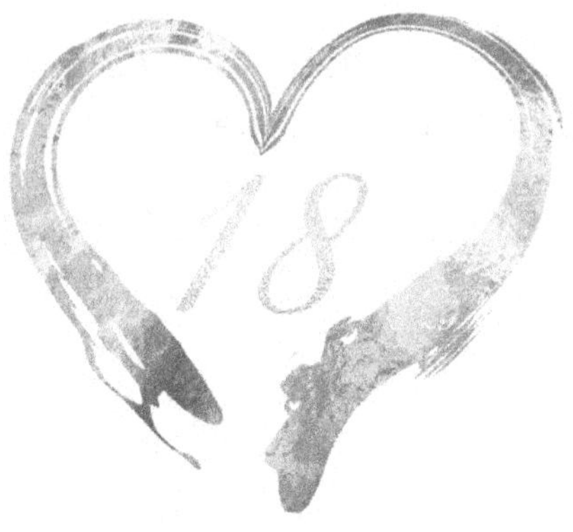

Shane

We'd just pulled up to my party, and the way Olivia was looking had a nigga ready to skip this damn party. I had to keep my cool because I was ready to fuck the shit out of Olivia.

I hired a driver for tonight because I knew I would be drinking, and I didn't want to worry about how much I drank because I had to drive.

Olivia did something new to her hair, and I loved it, and the dress she was wearing was everything.

The party was being held at Collingswood's grand ballroom.

I got out of the car and opened the door for Olivia. We linked elbows and walked inside. From the looks of things, it looked like everyone who was invited was already here.

My party started at 6 p.m., but I decided to be late. I wanted to make a grand entrance, and I was doing just fine alone, but with Olivia on my arm, my entrance was more than grand. I was rocking a royal blue custom-made dress shirt with a pair of custom white pants and a pair of royal blue Stacey Adams. I had on diamond cuff links. I was on my grown man shit tonight.

The crowd clapped their hands as me and Olivia walked in, and some were yelling happy birthday. We walked over to the table that my mom, Shyann, and Ricky were sitting at.

"Well, look who finally decided to show up for their own party," Shyann stated.

"You know damn well I wasn't going to be on time. I had to make a grand entrance. But anyway. Everyone, this is Olivia. Olivia, this is my mom, Sandra, my sister, Shyann, and my best friend, Ricky."

"Hello, everyone. It's nice to meet you."

"Hello, Olivia. It's nice to meet you as well. I love that dress," my mom said.

"Thank you."

The two of us took our seats, and I could see the surprised looked on my mom's and sister's faces. I have never brought another woman around my family besides Katrina, and that was honestly by default. If I didn't get her pregnant, she would have never met my family.

The setup was tight and to perfection. Whoever set this up was good at their job, and I wouldn't mind using them for all of my events. The servers started bringing out the food and drinks. My table was the first table to get served. Once everyone was served, we started eating.

I noticed Shyann's best friend, Bree, walking over to the table. That girl has had a crush on me for years, but I would never fuck around with her. For one, she was young, and she was my sister's best friend. That was no-no for me. In my opinion, siblings and best friends were off-limits.

"Hello, happy birthday, Shane. You look cute—"Bree said, but she cut her sentence short when she saw my date. "Olivia?"

"Hey, Bree. This is a small world. I had no idea that we were going to the same event," Olivia replied.

"Right. I didn't know you knew them."

"Well, Shane and I are good friends. I'm also Layla's teacher," she said.

"Oh, okay. I met Olivia today at my salon. I was the one who hooked her hair up."

"That shit bang, bestie. Come sit next to me," Shyann said, inviting Bree to our table.

We all shared small talk while we ate.

"Hello. I just wanted to know if everything was to your liking?" I heard a voice say.

I looked up, and it was who I assumed was the event planner. I stood up from the table to shake her hand.

"Yes, everything is great. Actually, I would like to use you for any events that I have in the future. You did a great job," I told her.

I noticed that she and Olivia were looking at one another oddly, but I would ask Olivia a little later what that was about.

"Thank you," she replied. "Hi, Olivia. Can we talk?" the lady asked.

"Latrisha, now is not the time or the place. I asked you to never say anything to me again if you were to see me. Excuse me, everyone. I need some air," Olivia said, and got up from the table.

I didn't know what the hell was going on, but I didn't like the way Olivia looked.

"I'll be right back," I told my family as I excused myself from the table so I could go find Olivia and see what was up.

I walked outside, and Olivia wasn't in front of the building, so I walked to the side of the building and found her there crying.

"Olivia, what's going on? Why are you out here crying?"

"Oh, God, Shane. I didn't want you to see me like this. It's your birthday, and you should be in there with your family."

"Olivia, you're my only concern right now, so tell me what's going on." I grabbed Olivia's hand and rubbed the back of it.

"That was her. That's Latrisha, my ex-best friend who fucked my husband and got pregnant."

At first, I didn't know what to say. This shit was crazy that the event planner was the chick I have heard so much about.

"Baby, I'm sorry that you had to see her here. If I would have known, she would have never been hired. She came highly recommend, so I thought she was cool."

"Baby, it's not your fault. You didn't know, and she is good at her job. She was the one who did my wedding, so I don't blame you for using her. She's a dedicated worker. She's just not a good friend."

"I know that I shouldn't say this right now, but what the hell was you your husband thinking cheating with her? She doesn't have shit on you."

We both just shared a laugh.

"Come on, let's go celebrate your birthday. I'm sure everyone is waiting on you." Olivia grabbed my hand, and we proceeded to walk back into the building.

"Liv, don't let anyone see you sweat. When we get back in there, I want your head held high, and I want you to be the boss bitch that you are."

When we got back in the building, the DJ had it rocking in here. I guess people couldn't wait to get their dance on. Olivia went straight to the bar to get something to drink.

About two drinks later, Olivia was on the dance floor with Shyann and Bree, dancing and having a great time. I couldn't believe she was being so free, but I liked it. I've never seen this side of her before; it was a joy to watch.

I sat at the table with Ricky and my mom.

"So you're in love, huh, son?" my mom asked, breaking me from my thoughts.

"Nah, I like her a lot, but being in love is a bit of a stretch."

"I think it's the perfect word for it. When you walked in here with her on your arm, your face was light up. I've been watching how you interact with her and cater to her every need. Instead of being out there on the dance floor with her, you're over here watching her because you enjoy watching her have fun," my mom said.

The shit was crazy because she was dead on about everything, except the part about me being in love. I didn't think I was to that point yet. I think I might fall in love with her one day, though.

"I know she's fine as hell," Ricky chimed in.

"Stop looking at my girl," I said, not meaning to let that slip out.

"Your girl, huh? I think she's a beautiful woman. A little too old for you, but you're grown, so do what you please. Just be careful, Shane. If you're serious about her, bring her by for Sunday dinner so she and I can have a heart-to-heart."

"A'ight, Mom. I'll see what she says. But she may

not agree because we're not like that. We're just friends," I told her once again, but she wasn't trying to hear me.

"Look, boy, just do what I say. I need to make sure she's on the up and up and have good intentions with you. I don't care that you just turned twenty-five years old. You're still my baby, and you're my only son."

I didn't bother to say anything else because nothing I said mattered right now. I got up and joined Olivia, Shyann, and Bree on the dance floor. If I couldn't do anything else, I could dance my ass off.

"Twerk" by City Girls was on, and the girls were on the floor showing their asses, so I figured why not join them.

I got on the dance floor and got behind Olivia. To my surprise, she started throwing her ass back on my dick, matching my rhythm. The crowd surrounded us yelling out all kinds of shit, which only made us go harder. Three songs later we were tired and needed to take a break. I sat down in a chair, and Olivia sat on my lap and faced me.

"I didn't know you could dance," she expressed.

"Yeah, I can dance a little bit, but I didn't take you as a dancer. You were showing your ass."

"I used to love dancing. It's just been a minute

since I've felt so free. I'm glad I came out tonight. I had a great time."

"I'm glad that you came out too. Thank you."

"No thanks needed. Let's get out here of here," she whispered, and that was all I needed to hear.

I got up and said my goodbyes, and the two of us headed out the door.

Olivia

As soon as me and Shane got in the car, we went at it like two teenagers in high school. I wasn't sure if it was the alcohol, or if these were my true feelings, but I was ready to give him the pussy right here in the backseat.

The car came to a stop, and we were at Shane's house. I fixed myself up to walk into the house. As soon as the door closed, we went at it. Shane started stripping me out of my clothes, never breaking the kiss. I could feel my pussy pulsating in my panties. I've never been so anxious to get dick like this in my life.

Once I was completely naked, Shane took a long look at my body and licked his lips. He led me to his bedroom and threw me on the bed. He placed his mouth over my exposed breasts, causing me to moan loudly. His tongue flickered over my nipples at a fast pace. I swear I felt like I was on the verge of cumming.

Shane made a trail of kisses down my body until he reached my center. He then positioned himself and began to devour my sweet nectar.

"Oh, God, Shane…this feels so good!" I moaned loudly. I tried to back away from his mouth, but he grabbed my legs and pulled me back.

"Stop running and take this shit; cum in my mouth," he demanded.

It didn't take me long to cum.

"Oh, God, I'm cumming!" I screamed.

Once I was finished cumming, Shane got up and kissed me hungrily before taking off his clothes, revealing his full, thick erection. I couldn't believe this young boy was packing that kind of dick. After Shane slid a condom on, he didn't waste any time fucking me. He wasn't making love to me as I used to. He was giving me straight dick.

I couldn't let him out fuck me, so I started fucking him back, trying to match his strokes, but I failed tremendously. Shane was hitting spots I didn't even know existed. I moaned and called out shit that I've never said before.

He flipped me over while still being inside of me and started hitting it from the back. I attempted a second time to fuck him back. I threw my ass back on his dick, matching his thrusts. The sounds of my ass slapping on his dick had me ready to cum.

"Damn, this pussy good. I swear you bet not give my pussy away. This my pussy now! Whose pussy is this?"

"It's yours!" I told him, on the verge of cumming.

"Did I tell you to cum yet? he asked, smacking my ass.

"No, baby!" I cooed.

"You cum on this dick when I tell you too."

Shane pulled out of me mid-stroke, then put me on my side and started stroking me while playing with my nipples. From there, it was over. He hit a spot that had me cumming like Niagara falls. It felt like I was pissing myself; that's how much it was.

"Oh, fuck, Shane, I'm cumming!"

"Me too, ma." He groaned as we both came

together. Shane rolled over and put me on his chest. I lay there as he played in my hair. "You got some good pussy, ma. I don't know how a nigga could cheat on pussy that good," he said, causing me to smile.

Nothing else was said. We just lay there in the dark until we both fell asleep.

***

I spent the entire weekend with Shane, and I was having the time of my life. The sex he was giving me was something I've never experienced in my life. Shane was giving me the best dick of my life.

I mean, I had good sex with Andrew, but I was having the best sex of my life with Shane. If I wasn't careful, I could be easily be turned out or dick whipped, as they call it.

Tonight, I was going over to his mom's place for dinner. To say I was nervous was an understatement. She seemed pretty cool at the party, and I could tell that Shane, his mom, and sister were close-knitted.

I didn't feel like dressing up, so a pair of jeans and a shirt would have to do. After getting dressed, I drove over to Shane's mom's house for dinner. After parking, I rang the bell, and Shane answered the door. He greeted me with a kiss on my lips before taking me to the kitchen where his mom was located.

"Good evening, Ms. Hill," I spoke when I walked into the kitchen.

"Hey, baby. How are you? Dinner will be ready in a minute."

"I'm well. How are you?"

"I'm good, baby. Thanks for coming over to chat with me. Dinner will be ready in a minute," she said with a bright smile.

Dinner wasn't bad at all. In fact, I enjoyed it. Once we were finished with dinner, Ms. Hill asked if she could speak with me alone. Shane got up and left the room, leaving me alone with his mother. The nerves in my stomach were doing backflips.

"Look, honey. I'm going to get straight to the point. I can see that my son is in love with you, so I would like to know what your intentions are with him? You seem like a nice woman, but I need to make sure that my son doesn't get hurt."

I thought about her question, and I honestly didn't have an answer. The truth was, I just having fun and was nowhere near in love. I was technically stilled married and nowhere near ready to be in a relationship.

"If I could be honest, I, at the moment, I don't

have any intentions. I like your son a lot, and he's helped me through one of the most difficult times in my life. But I'm not in love with Shane, and I don't think he's in love with me either."

"I appreciate your honesty about your intentions, but that's not good enough for me. And trust me, I know my son, and he's in love with you. And by your answer, he will also be heartbroken. If you're not interested in my son the way he's interested in you, then maybe you should leave my son alone."

I felt so stupid for being here right now. I wished I would have gone with my gut the first time and not went to his party and met his family. I knew I wasn't ready for this, yet I still led him on. I'd just spent the entire weekend fucking him. Now how do I tell him that I couldn't deal with him anymore because his mom was right?

"With all due respect, your son is grown and is very much capable of making his own decisions. Shane is aware of how I feel and why I feel the way I do. I'm not trying to hurt your son. I'm just not in a position to be with him right now," I told her honestly.

"What does that mean? Please don't tell me that you're married?"

"I am, but my divorce will be final next week—" I said, but she cut me off.

"Oh, hell no. I don't want you seeing my son anymore. Shane, bring your ass in here right now!" she yelled.

Shane walked into the kitchen and looked at us. I guess he could tell that shit was tense in here.

"What happened? Why is y'all looking like that? Liv, are you okay?"

I was about to respond, but his mom cut me off.

"Why are you seeing this married woman? It's bad enough she's older than, you but married? Shane, I don't want you to see her anymore. She's going to break your heart."

"Mom, you are being extremely rude. What we have going on is none of your business. She will only be married until next week. I know what I'm doing, Mom."

"I don't think you do, Shane."

"I'm just going to go. Thanks for having me over, and Shane, your mom is right. I should have never dragged you into my mess," I said, walking out of the kitchen.

I could feel the tears welling up in my eyes, but I just needed to wait until I got to my car to let them fall. As soon as I got in my car, I drove off. While I was driving, I saw a parking lot and decided to pull in it. I put the car in park and cried my eyes out.

My life was a mess, and I had to be crazy to let Shane convince me that I would be okay. I was fucked up, and I needed a fresh start, and that's exactly what I planned to do: start all over.

Shane

Shit has been crazy since the night we had dinner with my mom two weeks ago. I haven't seen or heard from Olivia since that night, and I was losing my mind over it.

Layla had a new teacher because Olivia resigned due to personal reasons. I went past the hotel she was staying at, and the staff informed me that she'd checked out. I wasn't sure where she went, but I was worried out of my mind.

"Shane, you really need to talk to your mom.

This shit seems weird that you not fucking with your mom over some chick," Ricky said.

"Look, I'm good on my mom right now. She was way out of line, not to mention, rude as hell to Olivia."

I could tell he wanted to cry, but she should have stayed out of it.

"Shane, I'm not saying that Mom was right for how she went about it, but I understand where she was coming from. You're her only son, and she didn't want to see you hurt. Honestly, you were falling for her before she was even divorced.

"That woman is hurting, and she just needs some time to heal. Bro, if it's meant for the two of you to be together, then it will happen. I know that you feeling her, but we're young. There are a million women in the world."

"I don't want a million women; I want *her*. Let's just forget about it. I don't feel like talking about it anymore," I told him, dismissing the conversation.

I wasn't beat for my mom right now. I knew Olivia wasn't in love with me yet, and I was cool with that. Hell, I knew I was into her, but I didn't feel like I was in love either.

Outside of not being able to find Olivia, business was booming, and the money was coming in big time.

I couldn't have been happier to be making this type of money the legal way, and I didn't even have to do any hands-on work. Our business worked for us, so this was a good move to make.

In a few days, I was going to DC for Shyann's graduation. I was surprised when she told me she already landed a job, but I was happy for her, nonetheless.

Ricky had just finished rolling a blunt, and I couldn't wait to smoke. It seemed like I've been smoking a lot more than usual in the past couple of weeks. My phone buzzing broke me from my thoughts. I looked at the phone, and it was a text.

Katrina: *Hey. I'm stranded over in Philly, and I wanted to know if you could pick me up?*

I looked at the text for a minute before replying because I didn't feel like driving to Philly, but I also would never leave my baby mom stranded.

Me: *Where in Philly, Katrina? Just shoot me the address, and I'll be there.*

Katrina: *Thanks.*

After sending me the address, I got in the car and headed to Philly to pick up my baby mom. I was glad to know that my daughter wasn't with her because she was with Katrina's mom.

When I got to the address, I didn't see Katrina anywhere. I texted her to let her know that I was here, but she didn't come out.

Me: *Katrina, where the hell are you? I'm here.*

I waited for a response but nothing. I only planned to wait for another two minutes before I pulled off. I didn't even see her car out here. I reread the address that she sent, making sure it was the right one.

While I was on my phone, suddenly, the door opened up, and I was hit in the head with something.

***

I woke up and looked around, and it looked like I was in some type of basement tied up. My head was killing me. The first thing that popped into my head was Katrina. That bitch set me up. I swear she better pray to whatever God she believed in that I didn't make it out of here alive.

156

I had so many thoughts going through my mind, but the main thought was, why? I took care of her and my daughter. The house she lived in, I bought. The car she drove, I also paid for.

I heard the door open, and it sounded like someone was coming down the steps.

"Your punk ass finally woke up?" I heard someone say.

When I looked up, it was two dudes standing there. One was holding a gun, and the other was just standing there looking dumb.

"What the fuck do y'all want?" I asked, looking at both of them.

I didn't have an ounce of pussy in me. Although, I wasn't ready to die, because I still had so much to live for, but I also wasn't afraid to die.

"For someone who's tied up, you sure have a lot of base in his voice."

"Look, I don't know what you think you know about me, but you didn't do your homework. I far from a no one, and I'm not afraid to do die, so if you plan to kill me, then I suggest you go ahead and do it."

"I'm glad that you're okay with dying because killing you is something that I plan to do. See, you have money and a couple of businesses that we want. Maybe now would be a good time to introduce myself. My name is Rock, and I'm the one fucking your baby mom.

"Your precious daughter will be calling me Daddy from this day forth. You have to die so Layla can inherit everything. That will also help me and that fine ass baby mom of yours come up," this idiot stated.

I could already see these were amateurs.

I laughed loudly, pissing the dude off. "That's your plan? You're more stupid than I thought you were. Neither of you will ever see a dime of that money or my business. Let me help you out. I have a lawyer who will never let that happen because although Layla will inherit everything, she has to be thirty years old to do so, along with a few other stipulations," I said, then laughed again.

The smile he was wearing no longer existed, and he was now looking sick to his stomach. I could see the blood drain from his face. My laughing caused him to snap, and he hit me with the gun, splitting my lip, causing blood to leak.

"What the fuck is so funny!" he yelled.

"Your dumb ass," I told him, and he hit me again. The blood flew out of my mouth.

He pulled the other dude who was with him to the side for a private conversation. I could hear them whispering, but I couldn't make out what they were saying. He took his phone from his pocket and made a call.

"Yo, shit is going left right now. This nigga said she can't get shit until your daughter turns thirty. Now what the fuck am I supposed to do? You should've had your fucking facts straight. Now I still got to kill this nigga because he saw my face and shit!"

I felt like I was being pranked or something listening to these fools.

***

It's been a full week since I've been here, and I was feeling weak to my stomach. They were hardly feeding me, and I was naked, so I didn't have anything in my pockets to get my hands out of the tie. I wished they would just kill me or let me go.

The smell was bad since I haven't washed my ass in a week. I was never afraid of dying. I just didn't imagine dying this way, especially by being set up by my baby mom. I knew at some point that Ricky would find me because he knew I would never just disappear like that without saying anything. I just hoped that he found me before I died.

They were fucking me up every day and every time I said something they didn't like. I knew it was just a matter of time before I would die. I couldn't sit straight up in the chair anymore from being so weak. I lay here on the cold floor thinking about my daughter, mom, and sister. I knew they were going to be sick when they learned of my death, and I could only imagine how they were feeling knowing that I disappeared.

I hated knowing that my daughter would grow up without a father, and I wouldn't be around to protect her. The only thing that gave me a little peace was knowing that as long as Ricky was living, Layla would always be straight.

As I lay on the floor, I could feel the life draining from my body. I sent up a silent prayer to the big man above before drifting away.

Shyann

I was on my way back to my mom's house to console her. We were having a hard time not hearing anything from Shane in over a week. He didn't make it to my graduation, so I knew something was wrong.

I was missing my brother like crazy. Ricky said the last time he saw my brother, he was on his way to pick up Katina from Philly. We haven't seen or heard from neither of them.

Ricky said he was going to meet us at my mom's crib in an hour to discuss something important.

When I walked into the house, my mom was sitting at the table, staring out of the window.

"Hey, Mom."

"Hey, Shyann."

"Mom, everything is going to be okay."

"Shyann, you're brother has been missing for over a week. The chances of him coming back to us are slim."

"Mom, please don't talk like that. Shane is a fighter. I'm sure he's okay."

Before she could respond, there was a knock on the door. I opened the door, and it was Ricky and my niece, Layla.

"Mom-Mom and Auntie Shy!" she yelled, walking through the door.

After we hugged her tightly, Ricky sent her upstairs to her room to play.

"Listen, I caught Katrina trying to get on a plane. I had people at the bus stations and airports. I got her in a warehouse with my homies. I have a location on where Shane is supposed to be now. I don't know what his state is because I heard here's only hanging on by a thread. I have to go before it's too late, so I'll call you shortly," Ricky said, darting out the door.

Hearing Ricky say he heard Shane was in pretty bad shape made my heart almost pop out of my chest. My brother was my everything, and I wouldn't know how to live without him; my mom would just die. Shane has a young daughter, so yes, my heart was pounding.

I looked at my mom and saw the tears falling from her eyes. I went and rubbed her back. "Mom, Shane is a fighter. He's going to be okay," I told her.

"I just want my son home, and I want him home now!" My mom wiped her face when she heard Layla coming into the kitchen.

"Aunt Shy, I'm thirsty," she said when she walked into the kitchen.

I poured her some iced tea and just stared at her. She looked just like Shane. I prayed for her sake alone that Shane wasn't dead because I was sure that my niece would never see her mom again. Rather Shane lived or died, Katrina would never see the light of day again.

We waited around for hours, and we still hadn't heard anything back from Ricky yet. My mom was trying to cook dinner to kill some time, but I could tell this was taking a major toll on her. Plus, she was trying to be strong for my niece. We were sitting at the table eating—more so picking in our food when I heard the door. I jumped up and snatched the door open. It was Bree.

"Hey. I thought you were Ricky," I told her, closing the door behind her.

"Sorry. I had to come over here and be with y'all at a time like this."

"Bree, this shit is crazy. I think straight, I can't eat, or sleep. I want my brother," I cried.

Bree wrapped her arms around me and kissed my forehead. "I know. I miss him too," she said.

Loud banging on the door startled us both, causing us to jump. My mom walked into the living room as I was opening the door. It was Ricky. The look on his face caused me to break down in tears hysterically. This couldn't be happening to us right now.

"Where's my son?" my mom asked.

"It's not looking good at all. My bro is fucked up," Ricky said with tears in his eyes. I knew then if Ricky was crying, that shit wasn't looking too good.

"Oh, God, not my son!" my mom yelled, falling to her knees.

Andrew

It's been a few months since my divorce was final. I was trying my best to move on, but I missed Olivia like crazy. To pass time and help get over her, I've been fucking my assistant, Shyann.

Shyann was a pretty young thing with a bad ass body and good pussy. I knew fucking her was wrong, but it felt so right. It's only been a few months, but I was feeling Shyann. She made me feel young and vibrant.

We've been out a few times, but the situation with

her brother was in the way. She was always at the hospital visiting her brother. Whenever the two of us were together, we kept it about us and never get too personal. The only reason she told me about her brother's condition was because she needed to leave work a few times to go to the hospital or to pick up her niece.

I haven't even told her that I was recently divorced. I guess I didn't feel like we were that serious to disclose all of that yet. Besides, I didn't want to run her off.

I heard my bell, and I knew it was Joey. He was coming over tonight so we could do some sketches for this big company. I opened the door and walked back into my work area.

"Hey, what's up with you?" Joey asked.

"Shit, just ready to get this project over with."

"You and me both. So what's going on with you and the young girl?"

"Not much. We just keeping it light right now. Keeping it real, we just fucking."

"Is she any good?"

"Hell yeah. I'm getting some of the best I've ever had. Her shit is tight and stays wet. For a young girl, she got it."

"Damn, maybe I should get me one," Joey said with a chuckle.

"Man, I'm just chilling. I can get my dick wet and not feel bad, and I don't have no drama. I swear she's like a breath of fresh air."

"Let me find out you pussy whipped."

"Nigga, I wouldn't say all that. Can't a nigga enjoy good pussy without being whipped?"

"All I'm saying is, you sound a little turned out by the young girl."

"I don't get turned out; that's my job to do the turning out."

The two of us talked shit to one another while we worked on our sketches. We were up damn near until 2 a.m. and still had to be to work by 8 a.m. As soon as Joey left, I took my ass to bed. I didn't even bother to shower; that was how tired I was.

***

The workday was almost over, and I couldn't wait to get out of here. A nigga was tired as hell, but first, I had to stop by the market to grab a few things. A knock on the door broke my thoughts.

"Come in." It was Joey.

"You wanna go grab a drink?"

"Nah, not tonight. A nigga is tired. When I get home, I'm going to make something to eat, then take it down. We have a long day tomorrow."

"A'ight. Well, I'm going to holla at you tomorrow. I'm about to call up ole girl, Latanya. I need to get my dick wet. I've been all work and no play."

"A'ight, then. Holla at you tomorrow."

I got to Shoprite and picked up my items. I walked over to the fridge to grab some ice cream and ran smack-dead into Latrisha. I haven't seen her since all that shit went down at the bar and I found out that she got rid of my kid.

For months, I blamed her for losing Olivia, but deep down, I knew that wasn't the case at all. I felt like I owed her an apology. Not only did I ruin my marriage, but I also ruined a great friendship with her and Olivia.

"Hey, Trisha."

"Hey, Andrew," she spoke dryly and proceeded to walk off.

"Trisha, wait can we go somewhere and talk?" I wasn't sure what she was going to say, but I just wanted to apologize and try to right my wrongs.

"Andrew, I'm not sure if that's a good idea."

"Trisha, I know that I'm the last person you want to talk to, but I just want to get some shit off my chest. I swear I won't be long. I just don't think that the supermarket is the place to do it at."

She looked at without saying anything—like she was thinking about it. "A'ight, Andrew. I'll meet you at the Collingswood Diner."

"Thanks."

I grabbed my last few items and checked out. I got to the diner in ten minutes. I parked the car, walked inside, and got a table. Moments later, Latrisha walked in and headed to the table.

"I'm not going to hold you long. I just wanted to apologize to you for everything that I have done. I should have never come on to you and put you in that predicament. I caused a lot of damage, and I can't do anything to fix that, but I can apologize for the part I played in it. I never meant for any of this to happen, and I damn sure shouldn't have expected you to keep my child."

"Andrew, this was on both of us, and I regret it every day. I lost a very good friend over some dick that I didn't even want. You took advantage of me when I was drunk, but anytime that we had sex after that, I was aware of what I was doing. But like you said, there's nothing either of us can do about it now. We both lost a great person over our selfishness, and now we have to deal with it. Andrew, I appreciate the apology, and I would also like to apologize for my part. Now, all we can do is move forward. Now if that was all, I think I should leave."

I gave her a head nod because she was right; we both already speak our peace. Trisha got up for the table and walked away. Instead of going home to cook, I just ordered food from there.

As I was eating, I thought about Shyann and wondered if she was okay. She had just got to work earlier, then suddenly, she had to leave due to a family emergency. I didn't bother to question her, but I assumed it had something to do with her brother. I wanted to call but didn't want to overstep, so I decided to shoot her a text.

Me: *Hey, love. I just wanted to check on you to see was everything okay. There's no rush to text me back. I just wanted you to know that I was thinking about you. Again, my prayers are with you and your family.*

I waited for a response, but I never got one.

After I paid for my food, I took my ass home.

Latrisha

Running into Andrew caught me off guard. I haven't seen or heard from Andrew since that night at the bar. And the only thing I wanted to do at this point was move on and start over again. I just wished that I was starting over with Olivia. I fucked up. I knew I would never find another friend as good to me as Olivia was.

After Andrew and I talked, I did feel a little better. It felt like a weight was lifted off my shoulder.

In the last three months, I have been working on

some big things of my own. I've been talking to this guy name Johnathan, and so far, things have been going pretty well. He booked me a party for his mom, and we hit it off from there.

We weren't official yet, but I didn't think it would be much longer before we had that talk. The two of us spent most of our free time together, and I enjoyed every minute of it. We haven't had sex yet, and I wasn't in the rush to do so. Sex seemed to only confuse things.

I told Johnathan everything that happened because I didn't want anything to come back and bite me in the ass. I needed a clean slate. Johnathan was older than me and was a chef with no kids but did state that he wanted at least one kid sooner, rather than later. He also wanted to be married, but I wasn't sure if I was ready for all that just yet.

When I got in the house, I kicked off my shoes and plopped down on the couch. I had boxes stacked up everywhere because I was moving into a new, bigger place. It wasn't too far from where I was already living.

My phone buzzed, indicating I had a text message.

Johnathan: *Hey, baby. How are you? I'm just getting off work and wanted to know if you needed anything before I headed in the house?*

Me: *Hey, hun. That's so sweet, but I'm good. I just got* *in. About to turn in a little early tonight. I have a long day tomorrow. I have this wedding to do over in Philly, so I need all the rest I can get.*

Johnathan: *Okay. I just wanted to make sure. Maybe tomorrow you can come over after you leave from your event and spend the night. I can run you a hot bath and give you a massage.*

I smiled at his text.

Me: *I think I'll like that. I see you tomorrow.*

Johnathan: *Sounds good. Get some rest. Goodnight.*

Me: *Goodnight. :)*

I loved that Johnathan always asked if I needed anything. He offered me massages and baths and never tried to have sex with me.

It was now the next day, and I was just about through with my wedding event. I was exhausted. I couldn't wait to finally lie down. As soon as I was finished, I sent Jonathan a text, letting him know that I was on my way to his place. It wouldn't take me long to get there because Jonathan lived in Philly, not too far from the banquet hall the event was at.

When I pulled up, I grabbed my overnight bag,

walked up to the door, and rang the doorbell. Johnathan answered the door with his thin pajama pants on and no shirt. Looking at his body, suddenly, my mouth went dry. I prayed that I could make it through the night without giving up any pussy.

I had seen him without his shirt before, but for some reason, tonight he was having a different effect on me. Maybe I was just horny since I haven't had sex since the last time I was with Andrew.

Johnathan was brown-skinned with locs. He had his hair in a ponytail, and I could see his dick print. Johnathan was tall with a nice body.

"Hey, beautiful. I hope you brought your appetite with you because I cooked for you. Your bath water is ready," he said, letting me in.

"I'm starving, and thank you so much."

I headed upstairs and took my bath. When I was finished, I went downstairs in my PJs. The table was already set. Jonathan made some seafood alfredo and garlic bread. It was something simple, but nothing he cooked tasted like a simple meal. After we ate, we went upstairs, and he gave me a massage as he promised.

Johnathan's hands rubbing oil on my body had me horny as hell, and I guess he was feeling the same way. He placed a trail of kisses down my back until he got to my ass, but he didn't stop there. He placed a kiss on my ass, making sure to kiss both cheeks. I let out a soft moan, and shit was on from there. He lifted my ass in the air and started licking my opening from the back. His licks became faster, and I knew it wouldn't be long before I came.

"Oh, Johnathan." I moaned.

Johnathan smacked my ass, causing me to bite my bottom lip. Before I knew it, I was cumming.

"Baby, I'm cumming!" I moaned loudly.

"That's what I want you to do."

After Johnathan finished drinking my sweet nectar, he placed me on my back and stared deep into my eyes for a moment before saying anything.

"I want you right here and now, but I need your permission," he said, never breaking his stare.

I nodded my head, granting him the permission he needed. He got off the bed and dropped his pants, and my eyes bucked at the size of his manhood. He smiled cockily and reached into the drawer on the nightstand and grabbed a condom. He slid the condom on and inserted himself into my wetness.

I closed my eyes and bit my lip in ecstasy. He was having a little trouble fitting his thickness inside of me. Once he was fully inside of me, and I adjusted to his size, the two of us explored one another's body for the next two hours.

When Jonathan pulled out of me, he took the loaded condom off and threw it in the trash. When he got back in the bed, he just stared at me with a serious look.

"You know from here on out, you belong to me and only me. Are you good with that?" he asked.

I nodded my head yes.

"Nah, I need to hear you say the words. A head nod won't work for this question," he stated.

"Yes," I said.

"Yes, what, Latrisha?"

"Yes, I belong to you, as you belong to me."

"That's all I needed to hear," he said, kissing my lips.

I wasn't sure if at the moment if I was in love or just turnt out by the dick, but what I did know was, I didn't want the feeling to come to an end. I knew for sure that I was dealing with a grown-ass man, and I was loving the feeling.

Shyann

With all the shit that has been going on with my brother, I needed a distraction, and I knew just the place to get that from.

After calling my mom to check in, I got in the shower and got dressed for work. My job was pretty easy, and I liked it, but what I liked most was Andrew. I liked him a lot, and he was a pretty cool boss.

I walked into work and clocked in. I set my belongings down before heading to Andrew's office to let him know I was here. I knocked on the door, and he told me to come in. I walked into his office, and he licked his lips.

"You like nice today, and I didn't expect to you."

"Thanks, and yeah, I needed a distraction. I've been sitting around crying all day, every day."

"I know that it has to be hard. How's it going?"

"Not too good. We have to remove him from the machine by the end of the week. But if you don't mind, I don't want to talk about that right now."

"I'm sorry. Let's talk about something else. Lock the door and bring your sexy ass over here," he said, licking his lips.

I walked over to him, and he placed me on his desk. He hiked up my dress, and a smile appeared on his face when he realized I wasn't wearing any panties. Andrew buried himself into my sweet spot and began to pleasure me. I threw my head back and bit my bottom lip.

"Oh, fuck, Andrew…" I moaned, grabbing his head. It didn't take me long to climax.

"Cum for Daddy," he said, in between licks. His licks became faster, and I was ready to cum.

"Oh, God, Andrew, I'm about to cum!"

After I was finished cumming, Andrew stood up and bent me over the desk before unzipping his pants. I watched him grab a condom from his drawer. After he put it on, he slid inside of me, delivering slow strokes at first. I matched his every stroke until the two of us climaxed together.

Andrew didn't pull out right away. He just marinated in the pussy. Once he pulled out, the two of us walked into his bathroom to clean up.

I fixed myself up and headed into my office. I picked my phone up and saw that I had a text message. I opened the massage, and it was from Bree.

Bree: *Bitch, you need to call me ASAP.*

As I was dialing her number, she called me.

"Bitch, wassup?

"You need to get to my shop ASAP," she whispered.

"What's going on, and why are you whispering?" I asked.

"Because I wasn't supposed to call you, but hurry. That chick, Olivia, is here, and she's pregnant."

"I'm on my way. Whatever you do, don't let her leave."

"A'ight, just hurry."

When I hung up the phone, I went into Andrew's office to let him know that I needed to leave.

"Hey, I'm sorry, but I have to leave. I have a family emergency.

"Call me if you need me," Andrew said.

I nodded my head and headed out the door. I was speeding down the highway to get to Bree's shop. Once I heard that Olivia was pregnant, I needed to talk to her to find out if it was my brother's baby.

During the ride to the shop, I thought about Andrew and how supportive he was during this troubling time. Andrew made sure that I was good every day, even on days I didn't work. The two of us have been dealing with each other sexually for about a month and some change.

Andrew was an older man with a little swag. I still didn't think my family would approve of us because of his age, which was why I haven't said anything yet.

Besides, I was still kinda checking for Ricky's fine ass. It was hard to be around him so much and not want to fuck him. That was a fine-ass man. I walked into the shop and headed straight to Bree's office.

And there Olivia was in the flesh. I could tell she was shocked to me, but not as a shocked as I was to see her.

"Hello, Olivia."

"Hi. Where's Shane? Would someone please tell me what's going on, and why did he send you?" she questioned.

"Look, there's no easy way for me to say this, but Shane is in the hospital. He's in a coma, and it's not looking too good for him," I told her with tears in my eyes.

Saying that shit out loud had me fucked up and emotional. I guess I wasn't ready to accept the truth.

Oliva's eyes widened, and she covered her mouth in shock. "Oh, God, no. Please don't tell me that. What happened?" she cried. "I need to see him, please?"

I knew my mom probably wouldn't be happy to see her, but I thought she had a right to see my brother, especially if she was carrying his child. Not to mention, I knew that Shane would want her there.

"He was beaten damn near to death and has been in a coma for a little over two months."

She just stood there crying. I felt bad for her.

"Is it true that you're pregnant by my brother?"

"Yes. That's the only reason I came back so I could tell him. I moved to New York when I left," she answered.

"Let's go, but I need you to know something. Shane doesn't look like himself."

I was glad Bree called me. Otherwise, we might not have ever known about the baby.

The two of us headed out of the shop after I thanked Bree for calling me. I got in my car and pulled off with Olivia following behind me.

C a u g h t   U p   i n   a   T h u g ' s   H e a r t

Ricky

I'd just got to the warehouse where I was keeping Katrina and her little boyfriend. They were responsible for the condition my boy was in. I wanted to kill Katrina, but I was praying to God that Shane pulled through, so we could kill these motherfuckers himself.

We just went legit, and now I was pulled back into this street shit. Katrina's parents have been looking for her, but the only thing they could tell the cops was that she picked up Layla and said that she was going out of town for a while.

Of course, they wanted to know how we got Layla. That was easy. We told them that she asked me to get her and bring her to her grandma's house. Katrina told the cops exactly that, which was true. I just left out the part about her having a gun pointed at her side when I made her tell Layla to come with me.

When I walked inside the warehouse, Katrina was crying.

"Please let me go. I'm sorry. It was all Rocks' idea," she cried, blaming everything on her boyfriend.

"Nah, you gonna die in this bitch, so you might as well just get the idea of you leaving this place alive out of your mind."

"Ricky, please! I'm sorry! I don't want to die!" she pleaded. "If you let me go, I swear I'll leave town and never come back. I won't even come back for Layla."

"Shut that bitch up," I told one of the guards I had watching them.

Shon walked over and smacked that bitch so hard that she flew out of the chair. He sat her back up and then smacked her again. She had blood pouring out of her mouth.

"Look, I just came to give y'all a break. Be back in two hours because I have to go to the hospital," I told Shon.

Everyone left, and it was just me sitting here. I thought back to the day I found Shane.

I got to the warehouse he was being held in, and I swear I thought he was already dead. He smelled horrible and looked even worse. His breathing and pulse were faint, and he was bloody as hell. It was visible that he was tortured and left to die. There were two men at that warehouse, but we killed the other guy on site.

I had four of my workers take Katrina and her boyfriend, Rock, to the warehouse, and my other two men dropped Shane off at the hospital and left. It wasn't like we couldn't tell what was going on, so that was the best way.

On the way to Momma Sandra's house, all I could do was cry. I broke down even more when I had to go tell Momma Sandra that her son might not make it.

They wanted us to take him off the machine this week, but it was hard. I knew we were being selfish, but as long as he was on that machine, he was still alive in my eyes. But once those machines cut off, then we would all have to face a reality that we weren't ready to deal with right now.

I mainly felt bad for my God-daughter. Layla cried for her mom and dad all the time, but she would cry hard asking was her dad going to be okay. It was one of the saddest things I had to watch.

Two hours later, the guards were back, and I headed to the hospital. I figured I'd spend as much time as I possibly could because it sounded like this was the end.

We always knew that we would die one day, but if I could be honest, I always thought we would die together. Shane had so much life in him. We were just getting shit together and getting on our grown man shit. I wasn't sure what I would do without my ride or die.

I was angry and ready to kill Katrina and the dude Rock. But I guess I was hoping that Shane would pull through and let him decide how he wanted to handle his baby mom. But what I knew was, after we take my boy off the machine, they both would both die a painful death.

My name is Ricky Smith. I'm twenty-five years old, and I was born and raised in Camden, New Jersey. I have an older brother on my dad's side who I didn't see. We talked here and there. He lived, down South.

As far as my father, I didn't fuck with him like that. He and my mom were never together, so I hardly ever saw him.

My mom and I never saw eye to eye, so I spent most of my time at Shane's house. I considered Shane's mom as my own.

I walked into the hospital, and she was at his bedside, like she has been for the last two and half months. Momma Sandra was there day and night. Most of the days, Shyann or I had to make her go home to get rest and eat something. I honestly believed this was even harder on her because she and Shane weren't on speaking terms.

I think that Shane was tripping a little bit over the Olivia chick. Shane was dead set on getting that woman at any cost. That was the first time in history I saw my boy so open by a woman. Not to mention, he hadn't even hit yet. Don't get me wrong shorty was a baddy, but I thought it was wrong timing.

"Hey, Momma Sandra," I spoke, walking into the room.

"Hey, baby. How are you?"

"I'm here. That's all I can say. These past few months have been difficult, to say the least. This is my day one, and now these people want me to process that I have to live without him. I don't know what to do or how to feel. I'm so numb."

"I know the feeling. This just seems so surreal. I'm not ready for this. I can't bury my son. I just can't do it, Ricky. At least if nothing else, I will still have a part of him here with me. My grandbaby is every bit of him. She looks and acts just like my son.

"The doctor just left out not too long ago asking if we've decided on what day it will be so they can make him comfortable. I told them I would let them know later because I needed to talk to the family first."

"Damn, speaking of family, where's Shy at?"

"She went into work. She said she needed to do something to help her take her mind off this."

"Yeah, I understand that. If you don't mind, can I have five minutes alone with Shane?"

"Sure. I'm going to go get some coffee and text Layla's teacher to see how my grandbaby is doing," she said, getting up to leave.

Once the door closed, I sat down at Shane's bedside.

"Hey, bro. I'm not sure if you can hear me or not, but I wanted to tell you that we need you, man. I need you. It's not the same without you, bro. Just know that no matter what happened, justice will be served. Believe that.

"Ever since we were kids, we've never gone a day without speaking to one another, so this here is torture for me. I wouldn't wish this type of pain on anyone. I dun' cried so many nights. I don't fuck with anyone else, so I don't have anyone to lean on.

"I'm begging you to fight and pull through for us. Mom, Shyann, and most importantly, Layla needs you, man. I know what the doctors are saying, but I believe in God, and I believe that you can do this. I love you, man, for real," I told him as the tears poured down my face.

The door opened up, and I looked up. To say I was shocked to see the Olivia chick would be an understatement.

Katrina

I lay here in the warehouse crying my eyes out every day. I was just ready to die already. Because at this point, I didn't have a reason to live anymore. I fucked up in the worst way ever when I double-crossed Shane.

I was just mad because I was in love with Shane, but he didn't share those kinds of feelings with me. It was mainly because of my mouth and how I would act every time we fucked. Shane had some great dick, and I was tripping off it every time he hit it.

I've been seeing this guy, Rock, for the past six months, and he convinced me to set Shane up, but that shit backfired on us.

I knew I would never make it out of here alive. I already felt dead on the inside. Someone was beating our asses every day but made sure not to kill us. I wasn't quite sure why not yet.

I didn't think Shane was dead, but I knew he had to be pretty bad off because he was still in the hospital two months later. I never wanted Shane to suffer. I thought they would have just shot him, but nope. They took things too far.

Shane didn't deserve what happened to him all because of me and my jealousy. Now my daughter wouldn't have a mother or a father.

When Ricky came in, I pleaded for him to spare my life, but he wasn't haven't it.

I lay there thinking about what my baby girl was going through. I thought back to the day Ricky found me at the airport.

Layla and I had just got to the bus station when I heard Layla yell, "God-Daddy!" I knew then that I was as good as dead, but I had to play it off for the sake of my daughter. She jumped in his arms, and she placed a kiss on her forehead.

"God-Dad needs you to go with my friend while I talk

to Mommy, okay?"

After she went to the car, Ricky made sure that we were where no cameras could see us. Ricky punched me so hard in my face that it felt like he broke my jaw.

"Where the fuck is Shane? And you better not play no fucking games with me, or I'll blow your fucking head off!" he yelled.

All I could do was cry. I was scared as shit.

"Please don't kill me, Ricky. I tell you everything," I pleaded.

I told Ricky where Shane was located and who was there. He then made me call Rock and tell him that I was about to board the bus and I would call when I arrived. Once I hung up the phone, he took my phone and walked off. I thought to myself that was easy, but suddenly, I was thrown in the back of a trunk, and when I woke up, I was in a warehouse tied up.

A few hours later, some guys walked into the warehouse with Rock. He was bleeding, and his eyes were so swollen that he couldn't see out of them.

Every day, I prayed that God would give me a second chance at life and let me live, although I knew I didn't deserve it.

"Can you please just kill me? This pain is too much," I pleaded with the guard who was watching us.

"Bitch, your ass will die when Boss say you can die. Now shut the fuck up before I put this dick in it. As a matter of fact, that's what you can do. Suck on this fat dick while your little boyfriend watch."

He told the other guy to hold the gun to my head as he unzipped his pants. He walked over and shoved his dick into my mouth.

"Bitch, if you bite my shit, I'm going to fuck you up. I won't kill you, but you going to wish you were dead."

The whole time I was giving him head, I cried.

"Come on, man. Is that necessary?" Rock said.

I knew they were about to hit him, but at least he tried to stand up for me.

"Nigga, shut the fuck up before I make you suck it too," he said, causing the other guy to laugh.

I swear I just wanted to die. It seemed like I was sucking forever before he finally came in my mouth. It was so much nut that I started to gag and throw up. I was sick to my stomach. The guys just laughed at the expense of my pain.

"I have to use the bathroom," I said, but no one took me.

So I had to lay there in my own piss until they decided to have someone come out, wash me up, and allow me to change my clothes. But I felt like that was only for their benefit so they didn't have to smell us.

I wondered what my daughter was doing. I would do anything to hear her voice one last time. I also thought about my parents. I knew they were worried as sick about me as I was about them. I didn't even know if they were even still alive.

Two months Ago

Olivia

I was lying here on the couch, watching TV, trying to figure out if I wanted to make a trip to Jersey or not. I kind of felt bad for the way I left without even saying so much of a goodbye to Shane or my students, and now I felt like shit.

I've been miserable since I left. I honestly didn't have any friends, and I thought about Shane every day, all day. At first, I couldn't eat or sleep, but as time went on, things became easier. I was just a bit lonely.

The only person I have been talking to from time to time was my neighbor and my therapist. I was afraid to make friends because I felt betrayed. I wondered how Shane was doing.

When I left, I drove until I decided to stop. I landed in New York. I had to admit, it was a little too busy here for me, and I wasn't sure if this was where I wanted to make it in life in the long run. I most definitely didn't think it was a suitable place to raise a child.

It was just about time for me to go to my therapy session. I got to my therapist in about fifteen minutes. I walked into the office and took my seat.

"Good evening, Ms. Monroe," my therapist said, calling me by my maiden name.

"Good evening, Dr. Blake."

"So I'm just going to get right into this. Have you given more thought to telling Shane about your pregnancy?"

"I don't know what to do. I thought about it, but I just don't feel like I should. I don't know what that conversation is supposed to sound like. 'Hey, Shane. I know I left without saying goodbye. I even got a new number and left my job to get away from you, but I'm back, and by the way, I'm two months pregnant with your child'?"

You heard right. I'm pregnant. I found out last month. I was in the bank, and out of nowhere, I passed out. I wasn't sure how I got to the hospital, but when I came to, that was where I was. They ended up keeping me overnight and ran a bunch of tests.

I didn't even believe her when the doctor told me that I was pregnant. As much as I wanted a baby, I always thought it was going to be with Andrew. Not some young guy who I decided to have a weekend fling with because I was going through something.

I contemplated for a month long if I should get rid of the baby and never speak of it again, but I just didn't think that was a wise idea. This was my first pregnancy in life, and I was thirty-five years old.

I still couldn't believe I got pregnant in one weekend. Yet, I was trying to get pregnant for an entire year, and it never happened. Me not getting pregnant was what ended my marriage.

"Ms. Monroe, you know I'm a straight-shooter with you. I understand that you don't like the situation or how it came about, but if you plan to have that baby, you need to tell the father. When it comes to raising a child, it's not okay to purposely keep a child from their father. You have to stop being afraid to live because of what other people may think or say.

"This is your life, and it's time that you start doing things for yourself. It's clear to me that you care a great deal about this Shane guy, but because of his age, you won't give him a shot, although you say he makes you feel like no other. Your homework is to drive to Jersey and tell this man that you're having his baby because he deserves to know. Plus, it will make you feel better, no matter the outcome," my therapist told me.

I knew she was right, but I didn't want her to be. His mom already didn't care for me, and now, I have to go back and tell them I was pregnant, but I still couldn't be with him? *What the hell did I get myself into?*

"Do I have to?" I asked, pouting.

"Yes, you have to. It's the doctor's orders. Olivia, everything will be just fine. I'll see you Tuesday."

When I left, I decided to go to the wing shop around the corner from my apartment. After getting my food, I headed back home. As soon as I got into the house, I stripped down to my bra and panties.

I walked by the mirror and caught a glimpse of my baby bump. I stopped and just stared at it for a little bit. This was the first time that I've truly acknowledged that I was pregnant. I put my hand on my belly and gave it a small rub.

"I'm sorry I'm bringing you into this mess," I said out loud.

***

Present Day

I'd just arrived in Jersey, and I headed straight to the hotel to check-in. After getting settled, I stood in the mirror and talked to myself about what I was going to say to Shane.

I wondered if he wanted to see me. I even wondered if he had moved on or not. I mean, he was nice looking guy with money and a big dick. Not to mention, he knew how to use it. I was ashamed to say this out loud, but Shane's dick was the best I've ever had.

The one thing I knew I had to do was look good, and I knew just the person to get me right. I just had to make her promise not to tell him that she saw me.

I pulled up to Bree's shop, and for some reason, I was nervous to walk in.

"Hey, Bree."

She turned around and looked like she saw a ghost. "Hey. It's Olivia, right?"

"Yes, how are you? I'm sorry for just popping up after being gone for a few months."

Her eyes landed on my belly, and she searched my eyes to the question that was going through her head. "Are you pregnant?"

I simply nodded. "I am, but please don't say anything."

"Wait, is it Shane's?" she asked like a light bulb went off.

"Yes, that's the reason why I came back. I found out that I was pregnant, and it's only right that he knows. But please don't say anything."

"Oh my God. I—I—I—you need to let his family know."

It was something about her statement that gave me a bad feeling. What did she mean by "his family" instead of her telling me to tell Shane?

"Umm, why did you say tell his family? Where's Shane? He's the one I need to tell."

A sad look came over her face, and I wasn't liking how this was going.

"Look, you should talk to Ms. Sandra. Come to my office," she said, leading me to the back of the Salon.

"Where's your bathroom?" I asked because I felt like I had to throw up.

She pointed to the bathroom, and I could hardly get to the stall before I started puking. I wasn't sure what was going on, but I had a bad feeling. Once I got myself together, I walked out of the bathroom and into Bree's office.

"Look, I'm not sure what's going on, but please tell me what's wrong."

"I know you asked me not to say anything, but I had to call Shyann. She's on her way."

I just sighed heavily before taking a seat. A few moments later, the office door opened, and it was Shyann.

"Hey. Bree told me that you were here and that you were pregnant, so I rushed here because I need to tell you something."

"Can someone please tell me what the hell is going on? Y'all are scaring me. Where's Shane?"

"Shane is in the hospital, and it's not looking too good. The last couple of months have been hell on us," she stated as the tears formed in her eyes. "Shane has been on a ventilator, and the doctors want us to take him off this week," she said, now fully crying.

The news hit me hard, and the nerves in my

stomach were doing backflips. I didn't have the words to say, and I couldn't seem to speak. It felt like something was caught in my throat. I almost didn't come, and now that I did, he still might never know.

"What happened to him?"

"He was set up and kidnapped. They were beating him every day and not feeding him or anything. He doesn't look anything like the Shane we knew," she answered.

The tears fell freely down my face, and suddenly, I felt defeated. I couldn't believe I was about to lose the father of my unborn child, and he wouldn't ever know that I was pregnant.

"I need to see him. I need to see him now!"

"I don't know if that would be a great idea for you to see him in that condition, especially in your condition."

"Just take me to Shane, please. I can handle this," I told her.

She just nodded her head. "Thanks for calling, Bree," Shyann said before leaving out the door.

She got in her car, and I got in mine to follow her.

***

The entire ride to the hospital, I was in utter shock. I couldn't get this crying together for anything. I guess between hearing about Shane and the pregnancy, I was an emotional wreck.

I pulled up to the hospital, and it seemed like the closer I got to the door, the weaker my legs became. All I thought about was Shyann saying that he didn't look like himself.

I waited for Shyann near the door. Once she made it to the door, we both walked in.

"How far are you?" she asked.

"I'll be three months in two weeks."

I could tell she did the mental math in her head. I guess I couldn't blame her for wanting to be sure.

"Wow, I can't believe that I'm going to be an aunt again. It's too bad my brother won't get to meet him or her," she said.

Hearing those words come out of her mouth caused me to be sick to my stomach. Once again, tears filled my eyes.

"I'm not sure why you came back, but thank you."

"I came back because Shane had a right to know that I'm carrying his child, and now, I'm being told that my baby will grow up without a father. I don't know if I can do this."

"I know it's not the same thing, but I can promise that you won't be alone, and you and the baby will be set for life. Whatever you do, please don't get rid of my brother's baby."

I didn't respond because suddenly, I was feeling like I was under a lot of pressure. When we got up to the waiting area, Shane's mom was sitting there drinking coffee, staring into space. I couldn't help but feel bad for her. I couldn't imagine being a mother watching my own son die. Although she and I weren't on the greatest terms from when we last saw one another, I still felt sorry for her.

"Hey, Mom. Are you okay?" Shyann asked.

When her mom looked up, she looked at me with confusion written over her face.

"What is she doing here?" she asked as if I weren't standing here.

I understood what she was going through, but I wasn't beat for the bullshit today.

"Mom, she's pregnant," Shyann told her mom.

Her mom looked at me for confirmation.

"Ms. Sandra, I know that you don't care much for me, but I didn't come here with the negativity. I only came back to Jersey to tell Shane about the baby. I haven't spoken to Shane since the night I left your house. I just ran because I needed a break. A month ago, I found out I was pregnant, so I came to tell Shane that he was going to be a father again. But now that I'm here, I won't have the chance to tell him, and our child will never know him."

I broke down crying. Shyann hugged me tightly as I cried. A part from me was glad I came, and the other part of me wished I didn't know because this was too much for me to handle.

"I'm sorry if I came off the wrong way. I was just shocked to see you here. And I have to ask just to be sure. Are you sure that's my son's baby?" she quizzed.

"I'm positive, and I guess I understand why you were worried about protecting Shane's heart. I swear I'm not a bad person at all. I'm just a woman who was in a bad situation, and Shane was the one who helped me realize my worth. I will forever be grateful for Shane. If it's okay with you, may I see him?"

"Sure, baby. Ricky is in there right now, but just go to room two-zero-three," she told me.

"Thank you."

As I walked to Shane's room, the nerves in my stomach were doing backflips. When I reached the door, I stopped and took a deep breath. I was trying to prepare myself for the worst. When I walked in, Ricky was sitting at the bedside. He looked up at me as if he were looking at a ghost.

"Hi. Do you mind if I talk to Shane for a little while?" I asked.

"Nah, not at all. I'm glad you came. Shane would be happy to know that you were here," he said, excusing himself from the room. I

hated how everyone spoke about Shane as if he was already dead. I walked over to the bed and threw my hands over my mouth at how Shane looked. He was so skinny, and his face looked like it was starting to sink in. I could tell he had serious damage done to his face, but it was healing up. Tears formed in my eyes, but I closed my eyes so they wouldn't fall. I grabbed Shane's hand before speaking.

"Hi, Shane. It's Olivia, I don't know if you can hear me, but if you can, I wanna say…I want to say that I'm sorry for running off the way that I did. I didn't say a word to you, and you didn't deserve that. Shane, what happened to you? I moved to New York, but I came back to tell you something important. Shane, I wish you were here to hear what I have to tell you. Shane, I came to tell you that I'm pregnant. We're having a baby, Shane. I'm almost three months.

"I don't want to do this alone, Shane. I don't want our baby to grow up without a father. I know things didn't go the way you wanted them to go between us. I was in a bad place, and you helped me, Shane. When I moved to New York, I started counseling. That helped me realize that I do love you, Shane. It took for me to leave to realize how I felt. Please fight for your unborn child—fight for you and me. I don't want you to die, Shane. Please don't die on us. Your family is counting on you," I cried.

I swear it felt like I was crying for a lifetime. For a moment, I thought I was tripping and thought I felt Shane's hand move. I felt it again. This time, I was sure of what I felt, and before I could react to what just happened, the machines started beeping all crazily, and the lines on the screen went flat.

"Oh, no! Lord, what happened!" I heard Ms. Sandra ask.

Doctors and nurses filled the room making both of us get out the way.

"Oh my God, I killed him! I killed him!" I started to yell.

The doctors damn near pushed us out the door. As soon as we reached the waiting room, Shyann and Ricky jumped up and ran over to us.

"What happened! Mom, what happened!" Shyann yelled in a panic, catching everyone's attention who was in the waiting room.

"Shane is dead! She killed him!" Ms. Sandra yelled, charging at me.

It was a good thing that Ricky was able to get her before she knocked me down. "Mom, chill the hell out!" Ricky yelled. "Everyone, calm the hell down. Shy, go sit and talk with Mom while I talk to Olivia," Ricky ordered, walking me to another seat away from the two of them. "What the hell happened in there?" he asked.

"I was talking to Shane, and after I told him I was pregnant, and while I was away, I realized I loved him, I felt him squeeze my hand, then the machines started beeping, and the doctors and nurses ran in and put us out. They said a doctor will be out to talk to us."

"Damn," he mumbled. "All we can do is sit here and wait for the doctor. I didn't know if my boy is gone or not, but he hasn't moved or blinked since he's been here."

"I know this may not be my business, but what happened to Shane? And how's Layla?"

"It is your business; your carrying his seed. And he would want you included. No one else may not know how Shane felt about you, but I do. My bro was in love with you. Between me and you, he and his mom haven't spoken since that night you left his mom's place. Two weeks had passed, and he still wouldn't talk to her. He blamed her for you leaving. Anyway, he was set up and has been in the hospital for damn near three months."

"Wow, what happened?"

"His baby mom set him up. Thinking that once he was dead, Layla would inherit everything, and she and her new dude would live happily ever after."

I sat and listened to everything that Ricky said. I felt sick to my stomach. I didn't bother to ask what happen to Katrina and the boyfriend because I knew how street dudes got down. Besides, I didn't want to know.

The four of us just sat here in the waiting area waiting for the doctor. I swear it felt like the longest wait in my life. I felt like I was going throw up.

Sandra

Sitting here in this waiting room, waiting to hear if my son was dead or alive, had me going through so many different emotions at once. I prayed, cried, and even pointed the blame finger.

It's been damn near a little over two months since I've heard my son's voice, and I felt like I was slowly dying inside. Shane was my only son, and he was my world.

It broke my heart when he stopped speaking to me all because I was trying to protect his heart from being hurt. Shane and I had never stopped speaking before. Shane called and texted me every day and made sure to visit me once or twice a week.

So when no one saw or hadn't heard from him, including Ricky, I knew something had happened to my son. I just didn't think that Katrina had anything to do with it. I just assumed something happened to both of them.

When Ricky told me he had a location on my son, all I could do was cry. I remember like it was yesterday when Ricky came to tell us the shape that Shane was in.

When he walked into my house, I could tell that he cried the entire ride there, and I knew then that my boy was gone. When I got to the hospital, I couldn't believe the condition that he was in. I could hardly recognize my child.

Since that day, all I have done was cry, and I've lost so much weight from not eating the way I should. I've spent every day up at the hospital until it was time for my grandbaby to get out of school. Between myself, Shyann, and Ricky, we took turns looking after her.

The name is Sandra Hill, and as you already know, I'm the mother of Shane and Shyann. I'm forty-five years old, but I still looked young for my age. I have a nice body and long hair.

I was born and raised in Philadelphia up until I

was about sixteen years old. When I was sixteen, I finally got the courage to run away from home because I was sick and tired of being raped by my step-father. To make matters worse, my mom knew about it, but I guess she loved him more than me.

To this day, I haven't seen or heard from my mom again. I didn't know if she was dead or alive, and honestly, I didn't care.

I was sitting in the waiting room drinking my coffee while Ricky had some alone time with Shane. I knew that Ricky was hurting just as bad as I was. If not more. I knew Shane and Ricky were extremely close; they were practically brothers.

Ricky was the last one to see Shane, and he was the one who found him in the condition that he was in. I knew if anything happened to Shane that Ricky would never be the same. The love of a true friend was a bond that could never be broken or explained.

When Shyann walked into the waiting room with that woman, Olivia, I instantly caught an attitude. I blamed her for the reason my son wasn't talking to me.

I knew she and I started on the wrong foot, and although I felt like she wasn't the right fit for my son, I knew that my son was in love with her, and it was nothing I could do about it. I could tell that she cared about him a lot, but I felt like she had too much going on for my son.

I guess that wasn't my place to decide, though. When Shyann told me that Olivia was pregnant, I was happy and sad at the same time. I wasn't sure if it was my son's baby or her husband's.

I walked into Shane's room and overheard Olivia talking to Shane. The tears filled my eyes when I heard her talking about the baby. Hearing her tell my son she realized after leaving that she loved him made me feel bad for interfering.

As soon as those words left her lips, the machines started beeping loud, and Olivia started screaming that she killed him hysterically. After they put both of us out, I lunged at her, but Ricky got in the way and took Olivia across the room, and Shyann pulled me to the other side of the room.

"Mom, what is your problem with Olivia? You need to give that girl some respect. She's carrying his baby, and he loves her, Mom. Shane is a grown man, and has the right to love whoever he chooses to love, Mom. This is hard on everyone. This woman just came back from New York to tell him he's having his baby, and she may never have the chance to tell him.

"Shane may never meet his unborn child. And Mom, even if Shane did die in that room, you and I both know that Olivia isn't the reason. They have been trying to get him off of the machine for quite some time now, and we had to take him off in a couple of days anyway," Shyann cried.

I knew my daughter was right and Olivia wasn't the reason for the machines going off.

"Shyann, I know that. This is hard for me, and I needed someone to blame," I cried to my daughter.

Shyann held me as I broke down crying. For the first time in almost three months, I broke down in public. I guess it was time for me to accept the fact that my son was gone. That was a hard reality to accept. I got up and walked over to where Ricky and Olivia were sitting.

"Ricky, may I have a word with Olivia, please?"

"Yeah, Mom. I need to smoke. If anything changes while I'm gone, just call me. I need to get high right now," he said, leaving the waiting room.

Shyann got up and walked out with him.

"Olivia, I know that it seems like I have something against you, and I just want to set the record straight. I don't have a problem with you at all. Honestly, I kinda like you from what I've seen so far. I just didn't think you were a great fit for my son with all age differences, and once I learned that you were still married, I became overprotective over my son. I knew right away that Shane was in love with you from the minute he walked into his party with you. I watched how he looked at you and the way you put a smile on his face. But it was when I watched him watch you on the dance floor…the look in his eyes was indeed the look of someone who was in love.

"Shane stopped speaking to me the night you left, and the last words he said to me were, 'He wasn't fucking with me until I made things right with you.' At first, I thought that Shane had lost his damn mind and that he was just talking out over anger, but two weeks later, he still wasn't speaking to me and then this happens. So I'm glad that you're here. Shane wouldn't have it any other way. I'm sorry for how I spoke to you at the house and here today. I heard what you said to Shane, and it was sweet. Thanks for allowing us to be in the baby's life. I have to be sure and ask. Are you sure that's my son's baby?"

"Yes, I'm positive. My ex-husband and I haven't been intimate in a long time. The two of us were on the outs before Shane came along. Your son became a great friend, and although he's only twenty-five, he has the mind and soul of a forty-year-old. He taught me a lot over the past few months that I've known him. He helped me realize that I deserved better.

"Shane and I weren't intimate until the weekend of his birthday. I had no idea I was pregnant or could ever get pregnant. I tried getting pregnant with my husband, and it just didn't happen. I never wanted to hurt Shane, and I made it clear I didn't feel like I was the one for him, but he begged to differ and told me that he'd wait as long as it took. Ms. Sandra, I'm not that type of woman, and I would never pin a baby on someone. If I weren't positive that Shane was the father, I wouldn't be here today."

"I'm glad to hear that, and just so you know, from here on out, no matter what happens with Shane, you will never have to go through this pregnancy alone. You have our full support. You're family now, Olivia, and if my son loves you to the point he's willing to stop speaking to me because I was in the way, then I love you too," I told her, leaning in for a hug.

She hugged me back.

"Thank you, Ms. Sandra."

"No thanks needed, and call me Mom or Momma Sandra from now on."

Just then, I looked up, and Shyann and Ricky were walking back into the waiting room.

"Y'all good now?" Ricky asked, wrapping his arm around me.

"Yes, we're good," I replied.

"I'm glad to hear that because we all have to stick together and be there for one another. And where the hell is the doctor at? I have to pick Layla up in an hour, and I don't want to miss anything."

Just as the words left his mouth, the door opened,

and the doctor walked over to us.

"Family of Mr. Hill?"

I tried to read his face, but I wasn't getting anything. The nerves in my stomach were doing backflips.

"Doctor, how's my son?"

"Ms. Hill, I'm so sorry…"

221

www.ingramcontent.com/pod-product-compliance
Lightning Source LLC
Chambersburg PA
CBHW061247120726
48001CB00001B/188